T0147688

Prior Praise

Manuscripts International Literary Awards Honorable Mention to Mr. Joe Perry (selected by a Washington State College judge for superior creative excellence)

"Mr. Perry has such a strong, honest, clear voice—so perfectly his own."
—Cynthia Candler, author and English Department chairperson of Herman Furlough Middle School, Terrell, Texas

"*The Homecoming* is a wonderful, thank-you kind of message and well written."
—Mike Melugin, television and stage actor and English teacher at Herman Furlough Middle School (his intelligence should be admired since he was smart enough to marry Cynthia Candler)

Prologue

The gold case of the old Rockford pocket watch lay open beside the growing stack of manuscript pages heaped on the old man's desk. Soft ticking provided a gentle rhythm behind the urgent scratching of pen against notepaper. The watch hands swept across the ivory face, as if to remind the writer that time was passing too quickly for him. And time was running out. Only fifty pages of his life had been written, and surely it would take ten thousand words to tell the whole story. He paused and glared at the watch. No, it was not the timepiece that was the enemy but time itself. The old man cocked a bushy eyebrow and tugged at his chin as he recalled how he had come to carry the watch, the heavy gold watch chain, and the California-minted, ten-dollar-gold-piece watch fob. It was one of the children's favorites—a tale they never tired of hearing—but the old man had not yet put the story down on paper.

His grandson, the one for whom he was writing, might never remember the story. His family had moved to Texas in 1951, and the boy had not been exposed to the story as much as others in the family had. And distance seemed to be a hindrance to real communication. The old man had held off writing the story as though he could bribe the watch and slow down the steady forward movement of its hands.

"And when I've written about you, old friend," he often whispered to the watch, "then I'll shut your golden case and send you to Joe to carry. I shall lay down my pen at last, and you may mark the hour of my passing as just another tick of your cycle."

The watch made no promise in return; it was as though it did not care if the story of the pocket watch and chain and fob were ever written.

But there were other tales to tell.

The dark blue eyes of the old man flitted to the silver, fist-sized paperweight that prevented the wind from scattering the legacy in the heap of papers before him.

It was the story of this stone that the old man now struggled to recount. The most important story of his eighty-six years was in that hunk of iron and nickel in stone! It had saved his life when he was twenty-six years old. It had given him the gift of sixty more years to live. God had used that stone to give him a longer life. It had made possible the sons and daughters and grandchildren to gather at his knee and beg, "Tell us the story of the stone, Dad Pauley! Tell it again!"

For sixty years, he had hefted up the stone and cried, "Well now, children, listen up! This may look like just a silver gray rock to you, but it's more than that. It isn't gold, but it's more than gold. This isn't any ordinary stone— no sir. This is a life-saving stone! Yes sir, you heard me right! A life-saving stone. Straight from heaven it came, blazing across the sky on the darkest morning of my life. It screamed down to earth and saved my life in a most miraculous way. It's the truth, and I stand alive here as witness to it. If it hadn't been for this stone, you wouldn't be here today because I wouldn't have been here to be your father or grandfather." This exuberant storytelling time was unusual for Dad Pauley. He was usually a quiet and dignified man, except when it came to relationships with his children and grandchildren.

And then his grandchildren would pass the stone from hand to hand. The eyes of the young and old grew wide at the story of danger and death and the miracle of the stone. Dad Pauley—not usually a very talkative man—would become almost animated when he told the story.

Perhaps of all the stories, this was the most often repeated. This was the most important tale to be written down because it had made all the rest of his life possible, but it was also the story that had not ever been completely told. He struggled even now in his eighty-sixth year with just how this story could be told.

The shrill whistle of the Danville-Madison train echoed across the towns between the mountains, interrupting his reverie. The old man peered at the watch a moment. "Late again," he grumbled good-naturedly, snatching up the timepiece and striding to part the curtains of the window in the bedroom at 212 Walnut Street he had shared with his wife, Lola Faye ("Loli" he called her) for sixty years.

Just above the silvery tops of the birch trees, a dark gray plume marked the progress of the locomotive. Far across the little town, the row of birch trees trembled and swayed as if to bow toward the train.

For a long time, the old man stood at the window and stared across the dusky fields at the birch trees. He had planted those trees as a younger man for his kids and grandkids to climb and ride. Too bad one of the fathers did not believe that small boys were created to climb and whoop and laugh.

Ross Perry would leave a legacy of harshness, of distance and cruelty, for his sons. It was for this reason that their grandfather, the old man affectionately called Dad, worked day and night on the tales of his own life.

Clicking the watch face closed, he turned from the window and returned to his task. Filling his pen with ink, he tapped the nib on the blotter. He much preferred writing with an ink pen rather than a ballpoint one. It was easier to tell the story aloud than it was to put it down on silent paper, so he whispered the words as he wrote at the top of the page:

For Grandson Joe from Grandfather Daniel B. Pauley:

Already I have written fifty pages, yet I find I have come only to my twenty-sixth year. This may be the most important tale of my legacy, however, since I learned how God delivers those who trust him from the miracle of a projectile. Read on, Joe, for it is a story you may not have ever heard. Perhaps one day you will have children of your own to whom you may read these words. Then you will tell them early what I have learned late: *A thousand shall fall at thy side, and ten thousand at thy right hand; but it shall not come nigh thee. Psalm 91:7*

Madison, West Virginia

June 19, 1978

Writings from the Columbine

January 1966 to January 1969

January 3, 1966

Today I took a rambling route on my way home from military work to our suite of rooms in the basement of Washington's most illustrious boarding house, the Columbine. Okay, I am writing sarcastically, but if you know me, you would understand that. I am sitting now in the master bedroom, trying to write about what I've seen and looking to our lavishly decorated bare walls for inspiration. Our suite combines a dining room (replete with table, chair, stove, ice box, and sink), living room, and bedroom (complete with large rollaway bed and sheet) into one large room. The stark naked water pipes running across the ceiling form a perfect prismatic design that is augmented by the peeling plaster of the dingy, white walls. But, sad though it may be, I must tear my mind away from these stimulating surroundings and try to record my thoughts of the sights I've seen the few short days I've been here, especially today. Steinke (my roommate from

1

the Land of a Thousand Lakes, Minnesota) is now on duty, and I am here alone. How shall I begin?

I arrived at Bolling Air Force Base to check in on Saturday, December 27, 1965. Snow had begun to fall, and it continued until seventeen inches had fallen. Gary had already arrived and had been sent to the Columbine. I joined him there, and we agreed it would be a suitable (affordable) place for us until we could get more permanently settled.

My first impressions? Washington DC is a hustling, bustling, busy, and rather detached city that is populated, especially in the inner areas, by lonely people. That's what I saw today as I sat on a cold bench in Lafayette Park and watched people, young and old, come and go. I had left my duty station in the basement of the White House and ambled over to the park before walking home.

A young man, perhaps a few years older than I am, sat beside me and began a conversation. "What do you like to do?" he asked.

I thought that was a rather strange way to start a conversation, but I answered his question by saying, "I like to look around and admire God's creation. Isn't this a beautiful park?"

"You're not from around here, are you?" he said. "If you were, you would realize this part of the park is known as a place where homos meet to pick up partners for the evening!"

"Is that what you're doing?" I said.

His negative reply was a relief to me. Identifying himself as an undercover police officer, he showed me his identification and badge. Then he advised me about the part of the park where I could more peacefully enjoy God's creation and not be bothered by men wanting my company for the evening. I still had a lot to learn about humanity!

In another part of the park, I watched the people who fed the squirrels and those who chased them. I watched arthritic old men who could travel well only with their eyes. I saw what appeared to be tears come to the eyes of the old as they watched youngsters play in the soft snow— perhaps tears of remorse for wasted lives! Maybe they were merely tears shed because their good times of youth and innocence were so long ago. Stony faces hid the crying souls of people black and white. Poverty, sorrow, and suffering know no special racial identity.

I saw busy people—people too hurried to do anything but walk through or around the park on their way to somewhere else.

I heard lonely voices crying in this city, lonely voices sounding like lost little children in a big store. These lonely voices came from busy people too disturbed to stop for a little while. The lonely voices filled my mind and haunted my memories! And what do I remember of the faces?

I saw lonely faces looking for the sunrise
Just to find another busy day.
Lonely faces all around this city;
Men afraid but too ashamed to pray.
Those faces fill my mind and haunt my memory.
But what I remember most is the eyes.

> Lonely eyes—I see them everywhere
> Burdened by the worries of the day.
> Men at leisure—but they're so unhappy;
> Tired of foolish games they try to play.

With my mind's eye, I will always see them—and I'll know God did not want it to be this way. What can I do about lonely people? Was another person in that park making mental notes about me?

I moved to Arlington, Virginia, on March 1, 1966.

Tuesday, May 10, 1966

I have two days off in a row, and I don't know what to do with myself. However, I'll do my best. I received Suzanna's letter and Mother's package today. I'll be known as a Texan for sure now. Complete with the Titches shirt. Titches is a famous Department store in downtown Dallas. I must write to Sally, Suzanna, Mother, my brother (Freddy), Jim Curtis, and some other friends. I guess I'll wait for a little inspiration so I can write something really interesting.

I'd like to just get into my car and drive down to Madison for a visit with my grandparents. I still think of their place as home. I can remember the layout of every room in that house except for their bedroom. I never had much reason to go in there. Funny, of all the places we have lived in Dallas, I can't remember the design of any of them. Maybe my grandparents are my compass, and I need to check with them to be sure I am headed in the right direction.

I hope that inspiration comes soon. Right now, I feel like Father Francis Chisholm of Cronin's *Keys to the Kingdom.*

I'd like to walk out my front door and just start walking and looking—trying to discover what's in this world with a feeling of complete freedom while I'm doing it.

I must write to Fred soon because he is about to embark upon a new phase or stage in life even though he doesn't know it. I didn't know it either at the time of high school graduation. Graduation is followed by the flowering.

Wednesday, May 11, 1966

We have relocated to an apartment in Arlington, Virginia, and our roommate works in Teletype maintenance. While we were moving in with Irv, a young lady from next door came to ask Irv if he had seen her pet. Irv asked if the pet was hungry, which I thought a rather unusual question until I learned that her pet was a boa constrictor.

I found out today, through Marv Cate, that they are looking for another man for Texas ranch duties. However, Marv has too much rank (they don't want an NCO), and they don't want another Air Force man. They already have an Air Force E-4. So, both Texans are out of the picture. First practice game tonight at eight against DASA, whoever they are.

I would like to get a good head start on the season, which begins next week. Somewhere within me is the desire to establish some better rapport with other WHCA military men (White House Communications Agency). Right now, I seem to be known as a rather slow but very accurate communicator—both in formulating and receiving messages. Perhaps I shall be higher esteemed if I establish myself as a good softball player. When I got to work, I discovered that I will probably be going to Chicago Monday through Wednesday.

Thursday, May 12, 1966

SFC Burnham called. Two navy men and I leave Monday afternoon on American Airlines flight 287 for Chicago. We must be packed and at the shop by 1600 hours on Monday. I wonder if the president is planning a trip to Chicago.

We won our practice game over DASA last night 13–10. Their pitcher had a lot of junk, and we had to adjust to his slow pitches. It was an error-filled game, but Clancy and Bodensteiner made real good defensive plays for us. I managed a walk and a single before Marv replaced me.

I will try to borrow Gary's suitcase for my trip next week. I'd rather not carry a trunk. Frankly, I have a little anxiety about this Chicago trip. I'm going with two of the best men in the communications center, and I don't want to make an unfavorable impression. If I do, this may be my first and last trip. Oh, well, all I can do is try to do my best and hope that's good enough. I'm only OJT (on-the-job training) on this trip—maybe they won't expect too much from me.

Friday, May 13, 1966

The Chicago trip is definitely on. I must go out to Cameron Station to purchase a piece of luggage. I will try to find a bargain. I must wait until I get paid for the Chicago trip before I send the car payment home. I better write Mom a short note to explain this.

Weather permitting, we have another practice game tonight. This one is against the 2044th communications group, and they are supposed to be pretty good. Same place, same time.

I must call my sisters and brothers before leaving on Monday. Who am I kidding? Long distance calls cost money!

Saturday, May 14, 1966

Last night's practice was a farce. Nevertheless, I enjoyed it. I found out the 2044th gets shaken up pretty easily. We made them throw the ball—and they threw it away. Herb and Wally pitched fairly well. We won 17–2 or worse. They tried to make us throw the ball also, and we threw out three runners from the outfield.

Muley got one at third base from left field, and I got two at home from right field. It felt so good! I also had two doubles (one to left-center and the other to right-center). I'll miss our first game Tuesday night. Wally says the team we play Tuesday will probably be our toughest competition.

Monday, May 16, 1966

I am packed and ready to go—almost. I hope I make enough money to compensate for the luggage I had to get in order to make this trip, plus a little extra. It would come in handy.

Wednesday, May 18, 1966

I got back from the trip at 1:00 p.m. I am tired but otherwise okay. I had to pay $8.50 per night for my room—plus extra money for meals—so I probably won't make much.

Because I didn't have any luggage, the trip shot a hole in my car payment. However, maybe in a week, I'll be able to temper bitter news with sweet. I expect a promotion by June 1. That means seventeen dollars more a month. When one has existed on ninety dollars per month for three months, seventeen dollars more a month sounds like quite a bit. Of course, our three months of subsistence pay will all go to the WHCU to pay for the loans we had to secure in order to have a few luxuries like food and housing.

Chicago is really a *big* place—part pretty and part of it pretty ugly. Hidden miscellaneous thought: *A man with too much pride is a vain fool, while a person with no pride is not a man at all.* I really believe that.

June 30, 1966

We took a trip to LBJ Ranch in the Hill Country of Texas. We left Washington at 1720, arrived in Dallas 1905, left Dallas at 1945, and arrived in Austin at 2025.

Friday, July 1, 1966

Crowley of 13A (Teletype maintenance for the White House) has taken me on the long journey through Johnson City. It was a ten-minute walking tour of the courthouse square, café, theater, bar, and general store. It looks like a miniature town that someone constructed of wood, sand, and rocks. The drive-in theater must have at least twenty speakers, and the screen is the back of a vacant house. The current attraction is *My Blood Runs Cold.*

My thoughts about wanting to be stationed here have somehow vanished. I don't mind making an occasional trip though—as long as there are friends like Albers, Furman, and Cate along.

Saturday, July 2, 1966

I've been working afternoons, and there was no traffic. What a dull way to spend eight hours. I guess we'll be here until July 11. How delightful! As I said before, I'm glad I didn't have to make this trip alone. I guess I'm not the loner people think I am.

When I got in around midnight, there was no one here. I decided to take a walk to Red's Bar to see if Wayne might be there. It's rather a weird feeling when the only noise you hear in a town on Saturday night is your own heels on the pavement. The place looked like a ghost town. I came to Crider's Motel and began to write my impressions of Saturday night in the metropolis of Johnson City where the Boss was born.

Sunday, July 3, 1966

This town sleeps through Sunday quite peacefully. It has no crime, no riots, no disillusion, and no trouble—and therefore no worries. However, it has no life either! And I think life—with its crime, riots, dissension, trouble, and worry—is still worthwhile because it also has beauty, peace, and good people.

But life is more worthwhile if you have people around you to help you enjoy living. You, in turn, help them enjoy living. Companionship and comradeship are good and indispensable.

This town is certainly good for one thing! A man gets so bored that he writes down thoughts that he's never been able to record before. He learns to appreciate the time he gets to spend with his friends (Wayne, Claude, etc.). Someday I will publish all these thoughts and have an underground bestseller!

I still can't answer my question. Is premarital sex right? I know it's enjoyable (at least I'm told it is), but is it right? Deep down, I know the answer. Why do I keep asking the question? People who engage in sex without being married to each other are involved in doing wrong.

My gosh. I'd better not write the rest of my thoughts. If someone should read them, they might get the wrong impression—or would it be the wrong impression? What kind of person am I anyway? I really wish I knew!

Maybe when I get through watching this television program, I'll go to bed and an angel or devil will come to me in a dream and say, "You aren't really such a lowdown guy. Sometimes anyway."

I turn into an iceberg when I try to talk to most girls. I need more self-confidence. But how can you have more self-confidence when there's nothing about which to be confident? For a long time now, I've wanted to reestablish contact and my friendship with Sondra. I hope a relationship develops. I must take my mind off her before that desire transfers to the far-reaching parts of my body. Once again, it is time for an addition to the "Jessie Pearson" collection.

The Time of Noon

When you're alone at night
And the old memories you call back
To help you do the things
That will put you to sleep
Don't work anymore
And even the aphrodisiac of magazines doesn't help
And there is no place to go, no one to call,
Try thinking about the sun.

The way it catches in the trees sometimes.
The way it follows you while riding in a car.
The way it plays in the hair of strangers on the beach.
The way it climbs hills with you and pushes you from bed in the morning.

Think about the time of noon
When everybody's just a little crazy.
Remember that the cliffs are white and steep

And you'll grow tired climbing them—
Tired enough to sleep, sleep, sleep.

I wonder if people consider it odd for a person to record his thoughts like this. Well, I must be myself no matter what people think—and if it's my nature to write my thoughts like this, then I must do it and hope that no one considers it odd or peculiar. How would they know about it anyway?

Sondra and I met at Fernwood Baptist Church in Oak Cliff just after one of my family's many moves. I attended Lisbon Elementary, and she attended Clara Oliver. Over months, we got to know each other better.

While we were in the eighth grade, she was voted sweetheart at our church's Youth Sweetheart Banquet at the Torch Restaurant in Oak Cliff. The food wasn't that good. This is not a slam against the restaurant. Our youth director had learned that the Torch usually marinated the chicken in wine before cooking it. Since we were Baptists, totally against alcoholic beverages, the chicken had to be fixed without the usual marinating. It was rather dry! When meat is cooked after being marinated, isn't the alcohol usually cooked out? I'm sure there is a scientific term for that process.

After the banquet, Sondra and I rode home in the backseat of her dad's Studebaker. I accidentally sat on Sondra's crown, and in addition to having a sore backside, I figured any future chances of a serious friendship were also nipped in the bud.

While we were in South Oak Cliff High School, our friendship was getting a little too serious for me. I was actually walking this girl to class and carrying her books! I remember sharing my fears with my best friend, Jimmy Curtis, and with a sly smile, he assured me everything was okay as long as she didn't ask me to carry her purse. I think he got quite a kick out of saying that.

Finally, I settled upon the normal solution for boy-girl problems in high school. I wrote her a note. The note was written on the back of a scripture booklet, the last quote of which was "Heaven and earth shall pass away, but my word shall never pass away." My words included the usual "this-is-just-getting-too-serious, let's-just-be-friends" message. I admit I was scared. I still am!

She was in the well-known South Oak Cliff High School choir, which was directed by Julia Dean Evans. She was the choir accompanist and could play the piano beautifully. Me? I was only known as the boy who sometimes made announcements over the PA system in Uncle Ben's office for the honor society or the Red Cross. I had a good radio voice—and a good radio face. Uncle Ben was our name for our principal, Dr. Ben Matthews.

Now I am off in the military and have received word from my younger sister, Suzanna, that Sondra is a student teacher at Kimball High School in Dallas. Suzanna is a student there. I should mention that kids in our family never seemed to attend the same schools. Why was that? Like gypsies, we moved a lot. My older sister, Sally, attended Adamson High School. I attended South Oak Cliff. My younger brother, Fred, attended Sunset High School, and my younger sister attended Kimball. Our oldest brother, Gene Bradley, attended Spence Junior High School and may have gone to Adamson. If we had any more kids in our family, Dallas might have had to build more schools in Oak Cliff.

Since Sondra is graduating from North Texas State University, and she is preparing to be an educator, she may not want to hear from somebody who wanted to "just be friends." When we get back home from the ranch, I think I'll send her a silly card and try to gauge where she is in her life.

Well, so much for my ramblings for today. I think I'll read until Wayne gets back. The girl he's taking home really looks like a nice one—and Maughan is right—her eyes are a pretty blue. Oh, good grief! Am I getting mushy?

Monday, July 4, 1966

10:30 a.m., and all is well. I am listening to Wayne singing in the shower. He really can't sing very well (neither can I, truth be known), but I can tell he's happy.

Thursday, July 7, 1966

Notes on the news conference:

- The president likes barbecue.
- Lucy is not a bad-looking girl, and she's not stiff-necked like her sister.
- Pat Nugent is not bad looking either.
- Newsmen like to eat and talk at the same time.
- The president likes peacocks.

Friday, July 8, 1966

I discovered that the communicator who referred to the president as "Clyde" and "Big Ears" when sending a test message back to the communications center at the White House when we first arrived is to be demoted in rank. It seems that President Johnson just happened to be monitoring communications in the ranch office at that very time.

I have come to find out that I don't really seem so out of place here. The ranch is very pretty, and most of the people here are very friendly. I wouldn't want to be stationed here permanently, but I wouldn't mind making temporary duty trips here.

I started reading somebody's book at the ranch communications center. It's called *The Sisters* and has some fairly descriptive sex scenes. Reading something like that can sure set you in motion. I'd better stick to *Look, Life, The Saturday Evening Post,* and similar magazines.

Saturday, August 23, 1966

I called Sondra at two o'clock her time.

Meanwhile, I am back at the ranch from August 12–15. Tomorrow, I leave for Denver. I should see some pretty country if I ever get out of the hotel.

August 16, 1966

Denver is a pretty city. Climate seems to be very nice this time of the year.

On Friday, after trying to call all day because of what Gary told me, I finally got through at about eight o'clock. I pried the news out of Gene and Mother. She is taking radium treatments for a slight case of cancer. Why is this family so secretive about things like this? I would much rather be informed than kept in the dark about things. How can I pray about something if I don't know about it?

On Saturday, I went back to Washington and arrived at Andrews at 0008 on Sunday, August 28, 1966.

Saturday, September 3, 1966

Today we left Andrews bound for Battle Creek, Michigan. We arrived early and are staying at the Howard Johnson Motor Lodge, a nice place, for $2.50 a day. We had mostly good weather for our visit. I met some nice, hard-working people on this trip—Mason, Bartone, and Meets seem to be the cream of the crop in transportation and radio. We landed at Andrews at 0315 on September 6, 1966.

Journal for Philippines Trip

Since I hardly know where to begin, let's start at the point of embarkation. We left Washington on Saturday October 8, 1966, at 1955 military time on a C-141. We flew first to Travis AFB in California, arriving at 2055 military time. We met some people from the agency (Camp David Section) I had not known. Mike Langley (switchboard operator) and Bert Ferguson seem to be very nice people.

We were at Travis for two hours, and I was grateful for the chance to be surrounded by open spaces instead of closed up in an almost windowless airplane. We left Travis for Wake Island at approximately 2255 and arrived at 0330 local time. It was almost a twelve-hour flight. We were at Wake for approximately one hour before taking off for Clark Air Force Base in the Philippines, arriving there at 0730. It was a six-hour flight. The difference in time between Washington and the Philippines is twelve hours. Four of us left the plane and headed for Manila with our equipment.

There is a beautiful volcano very near Clark Air Force Base that has not been active for a very long time. Hillside country surrounds this otherwise drab base and is a very luxuriant green. We came into Manila via a Ford truck driven by Ricardo Javier, a Filipino who is an employee of the US Embassy. To say it was an exciting ride would be an extreme understatement. After loading a bit of equipment and our luggage, we packed ourselves (Ricardo, two recording men, Wayne Dukes, and me) into the remaining seat space in the truck and took off on our trip to the Pearl of the Orient, Manila. I believe that Filipino drivers greatly resemble Kamikaze pilots of World War II. No one pays attention to the center stripe when there is one.

Most of the drive from Clark to Manila (sixty or seventy miles) was over the MacArthur Highway. It is in quite a state of disrepair, according to American standards. We traveled through quite a few small towns and villages, and one of the things that struck me most was that the few schools I saw actually looked just like the schoolhouses I'd seen in World War II John Wayne movies.

Many children that we saw were *hubad* (bare from the waist up), some were *hubo* (bare from the waist down), and a few were *labis hubad* (all over). Most of the farmers and other hard manual laborers were *hubad.*

As we approached Manila, we noticed a large flatbed truck that had gotten too close to the shoulder of the road. It slid over into the water-filled ditch on the side of the road. The occupants were pushing desperately on the back of the truck, trying to push it out of the ditch. I admired their spirit, but I questioned their common sense. It was like trying to push the Rock of Gibraltar with a rowboat.

Both sides of the MacArthur Memorial Highway were lined by ditches full of stagnant water—perhaps serving as irrigation ditches for the fields. Caribou (water buffalo) frequent these ditches, which are deceiving in depth. The ditches look to be two or three feet deep, but I saw a full-grown caribou surface and leave the ditch. I wouldn't use the water for swimming.

October 17, 1966

Today is my anniversary—one full week in Manila. It has been an educational week. Most Manilans assume that American men in the city are here from the Vietnam War for some R&R (rest and relaxation). For a price, they are quite willing to procure someone to help us "relax." How nice of them! Most procurers or pimps are cab drivers. I do a lot of walking. There are many Manilan boys working as shoeshine boys on the streets of Manila. There are at least three or four boys on every block, and they are quite persistent with Americans who like to keep their shoes shined. I think the Filipinos have inspected my shoes better here than my Air Force inspecting sergeants ever did.

Unwittingly, I became a contributor to the Catholic Black Mask (whatever that is) without even knowing it. A Filipino girl walked up to me, pinned a plastic medallion on my shirt, thanked me, and asked that my donation be in paper money. I gave her two pesos (approximately fifty cents). You're fair game here until you become acquainted with the various tricks of the trade. This is what I meant when I said it has been an educational week.

The Secret Service is going to have their hands full here. Filipino police are not trained in crowd control or use of firearms. The average Filipino policeman has five children and a wife and makes from 30–60 pesos a month (approximately $7.50 to $15.00). He must find other means to make a living, and corrupt ways and means often prevail. Philippine people are not compelled to respect peace and order. Therefore, if the Manila police try to control the crowds during the conference, it will be something to which neither is accustomed.

Communist Chinese frequently enter the country quite illegally (smuggling is big business here) or through legal ports of entry. There are now more than two hundred Communist Chinese agents in the country. The Secret Service is well aware of these and other facts and is working feverishly to provide the best possible security for the president. Perhaps I should not be writing these facts down, but no one will ever read this. The Secret Service is really thorough. They have to be thorough! I think I'll go see an American movie today.

This unique place never ceases to amaze me. I have just come from the Ideal Theatre, and the theater doesn't sell popcorn or cokes. I could not imagine a good movie, and *Dr. Zhivago* is a good movie, without the two. It costs five pesos ($1.25) for loge (reserved seat section between the balcony and the orchestra). This is the top theater in this big city, and it has only one phone, which is out of order. Perhaps I should write myself a little note here— and anyone else who ever reads this writing—reminding us that not every culture in the world does things the way we do them.

I'm getting my Father Chisholm restlessness again—and I want to go roaming around the city.

October 18, 1966

> *This is my quest: To follow that star, no matter how hopeless, no matter how far … to be willing to die so that honor, faith, and justice may live—to reach the unreachable star.*
> *—Man of La Mancha*

This somewhat inaccurate quote sums up what I think I am trying to write. This is my desire! Let there be no more human suffering. Let there be people with broad minds and the capacity to understand the inner feelings of others. We should fish for man with nets—and not harpoons. With understanding and tolerance—and not prejudice or maliciousness.

Almost two thousand years ago, there was born among us one to be known as the Prince of Peace. He came among us, taught the nations, redeemed the earth, and departed his mortality. His message is the source of a great belief—which I share—and which is for all men, among the glories of the earth. Yet man is such that having been shown, he often does not see. Having been taught, he often does not learn. Illuminated by the light of peace, he often steps into the ravages of war. Sadly, there is little in our long history to make us believe we are any closer to the kingdom of peace.

It is the history of wars that tells us each side always proclaims God to be with them. God knows God must get sick of all this crying out to God. (I borrowed this from a thought I jotted down on a napkin a few weeks ago while I was pondering our presence in the Vietnam War.)

We, the great churches of Christendom, condone this war. To go further, we sanctify it. We send millions of our faithful sons, friends, or brothers to be maimed and slaughtered, to be mangled in their bodies and their souls, and to kill and destroy one another with a hypocritical smile and an apostolic blessing. Die for this country, and all will be forgiven you! Patriotism!

Christ preached everlasting love. He preached the brotherhood of man. He did not climb the mountain and shout, "Kill! Kill! Go forth in hatred and plunge a bayonet into thy brother's belly!" It isn't his voice that resounds in the churches and high cathedrals of Christendom today— but the voices of timeservers and cowards. How in the name of God can we come to these foreign lands, the lands we call pagan, presuming to convert the people to a doctrine we give the lie to by our every deed? It's a small wonder we are jeered at! Christianity—the religion of lies! Of class and money and national hatreds! Of wicked wars! The church will suffer for its cowardice. A viper nourished in one's bosom will one day rise up to strike that bosom. To sanction the might of arms is to invite destruction.

Wow! I'm not sure what came over me, but all of a sudden, the words began to flow. They came to me as I was listening to my transistor radio in bed. I had to get up and write them.

Now that I have read over these words, it sounds like I am against the war and the military, but I am not! I joined the air force to serve my country! I am just tired of all the holier than thou rhetoric. What my quest boils down to has been simply said before: peace on earth, good will to man.

October 19, 1966

Our hotel is three blocks from the American Embassy. Seven or eight blocks away and stretching as far as the naked eye can see is Manila Bay.

From my window, I can see a construction site of what eventually is to be another part of the hotel. Construction methods here seem to be rather primitive when compared to procedures at home. I can also watch the activities of the workers who stay in the building at night from my room. When their activities become physical, I naturally find other things to observe. It is enough to say that construction workers here are really not at all different from those at home, especially in their manner of speech and dress. I discover quite a bit about human nature by observing.

October 30, 1966

I have today succeeded in doing what all the other people from the agency have intentionally swayed away from. I have finally formed some acquaintances with some of the shoeshine boys. They have discovered that I am not a rich American stuffed shirt—and I have discovered that they are not cold-blooded, money-hungry connivers. Most of them are very poor, and I fully understand that this accounts for their desire to shine shoes for extra money. I let myself try to understand them and found that it wasn't actually so difficult. They, in turn, felt that I was really sincere (as I was) when I talked with them and asked questions about them. And so, through tolerance of each other, we managed to begin relationships that could be friendships if I were going to be here longer. I think the Asian people (Filipinos, at least) want our money less than they want our companionship. They need our financial aid, but they desire personal friendships.

I'm not trying to write foreign policy. After all, this was just a case of having a friendly street corner get-together and talk. They gave me, without any thought of charge or exchange, some foreign coins as souvenirs. I could only give my sincere thanks, but I could tell that gratitude was enough of a return for them.

Later this evening, I had another interesting experience. I stopped to get a shoeshine from a young Filipino man because I had promised to let him shine my shoes before I left Manila. He talked continually while he shined my shoes and finally got around to asking me to "lend" him money. Of course, I have grown leery of such tactics. So, I did not answer. He continued talking, telling me his three kids and wife were starving and said he would take me to his "shanty" to show me. In reality, I was interested in seeing if this man would follow through with this degradation. So, I accepted his offer.

However, I took the precaution of checking my wallet (minus twenty pesos) with the hotel clerk before I left with the guy. He took me down the street and through a dark alley behind an apartment dwelling where he had apparently constructed his little shanty of wood sides and floors and a tin roof. There were three babies, a woman, and a cat inside the dim, candlelit room. While I listened to his plea for money in his shanty, I felt compassion and contempt for him. I felt compassion because of the terrible living conditions of his family and contempt because he would bring a complete stranger into his home and flaunt his ignorance and poverty, embarrassing his wife and kids for a measly twenty pesos. I gave him the money. Somehow, I'll be able to do without it. Later, I wondered if my feelings of contempt really hadn't arisen out of the way I used to feel as a child when church people would come to our house to look at our living conditions before deciding what type of help we could be given. At least this man was trying to take care of his family.

November 3, 1966

Our quick "secret" trip to Cam Ranh Bay—no worthy thoughts! Only those who were going along for communications reasons were told of the trip and that was shortly before we were to get on the plane. Of course, there were a couple of reporters who were allowed to go along with us. Part of our group, while on the flight back to Manila, was talking about requesting "hazardous duty" pay for the time we were in flight to and from South Vietnam, and for the two hours we were there. My opinion wasn't asked, but had it been requested, I think I would have shared that the ones to whom the president spoke are the ones who deserve hazardous duty pay—not us.

For "safety reasons," we weren't allowed to get off the plane while the president spoke. He is one who is also doing "hazardous duty." I wrote that I had no "worthy" thoughts because I really didn't think very highly of the idea of asking for hazardous duty pay.

We are ready to leave Manila and depart for home. I've spent many enjoyable hours here just walking through the streets, meeting people at the embassy and in the American compound, going to Corregidor, and golfing on a spot that used to be the old Spanish wall around Manila proper.

We have too much equipment for one plane. One of the maintenance men will have to stay behind with me and accompany the extra equipment back to Clark. From there, we will probably fly to Japan to join another part of the group.

November 5, 1966

I was wrong. We flew to Kempo AFB, which is around thirty miles from Seoul. We landed here just after noon and joined the men who were working on the communications setup. After scheduling security watches, I was free to wander, although the briefing cautioned us not to go anyplace alone. However, it seemed a shame for me to be so close to a Korean town without at least paying a visit.

This past afternoon, I took a leisurely stroll from the base into the town of Kempo. It was a rocky road —much like a West Virginia "holler"—without the tall trees to enhance its beauty. There is a certain majesty about open land that has not benefited from any of humanity's "improvements"—such as highways that destroy the land so someone can traverse it quickly. This land seems to say, "I am permanent. I do not allow mankind to change me. Only God can do that. I am strong, healthy, and majestic—and the people who live off me must also be strong, healthy, and majestic."

I found myself imagining what the people of Kempo must think about American intruders with their jeeps, jets, and cars. An old, familiar pleasant sound aroused my mind from its daydreaming slumbers and brought it back to reality. I was near the entrance to the town, and the sound I heard was the unmistakable sound of children at play in the schoolyard. As I walked, the sounds became clearer, and I knew I was getting closer to the school. I knew also from the fluctuating cheers and boos that some type of organized play or game was in progress. Then I saw it—an old red brick schoolhouse enclosed by a faltering steel fence just like some of the schools in Dallas. The athletic contest was a soccer game in which the ball was kicked somewhat less often than someone's shins.

As I watched this interesting game, I noticed a large troop of young Korean boys marching in formation through town, apparently quite proud of themselves and their brown uniforms. Their group must have marched earlier in the presidential review at the air force base.

My attention thus diverted from the schoolyard, I continued my stroll through Kempo. There were many small shops on the side streets of Kempo, and I think I must have visited every one of them for at least a few minutes. Most of the people were quite friendly! I walked through what I first thought was a residential section where Korean girls stood on the front porches and shouted, "Hello, American." I politely refused their hospitality. After a few such invitations, I decided this was strictly a business area, and I was not interested in seeing any more of the "business district." Why did it take me so long to recognize what is commonly referred to as a Red Light District? Maybe because I've never been in such a district in the states!

I was strolling down the middle of a residential street (another dirt road) and watching the people go about their everyday routines when I noticed a neatly dressed Korean young man who had stopped in the street and was watching me in a manner that suggested curiosity. As I approached him, I smiled, nodded, and said hello. To my surprise, he spoke in perfect English! He said he was Mr. Yang Shin Choi and inquired my name. Mr. Yang offered to show me through the town, and I very eagerly accepted his offer. He was a friendly, handsome, and articulate person whose friendliness I shall never forget. Mr. Yang took me to dinner in Kempo in what he said was his favorite place. I don't know what I ate and drank in that restaurant this evening. The only way I could distinguish between the food and drink, other than taste, was to remember the drink was in a small glass and the food in a large bowl.

After that, he led me through some narrow streets to a residence where he was renting a room. We removed our shoes before entering his room. For a couple of hours, we sat on the floor in his room, talking, laughing, and discussing. We discussed our differing cultures and agreed that each has its merits and its drawbacks. I felt so comfortable with Mr. Yang that I very much wanted to stay the rest of the night and sleep there as he invited me to do. However, I was scheduled to relieve Nichols at ten o'clock for security duty on the cold plane. I said good-bye to my newfound friend, and he escorted me as far back to the base as he could. He gave me his card in case I want to communicate. I think I shall.

So, we are to spend the night on this big, cold plane, keeping our equipment company. It's so cold that I don't think I'll be able to sleep. Muley is in the pilot's chair, and I think I will read the navigator's log until he awakens. The tune of Tchaikovsky's "Piano Concerto #1" keeps playing in my mind because Mr. Yang played it on his record player several times and kept saying, "It is much better to make love, not war."

We are leaving for the USA via Japan. After we stopped at an air force base in Japan—I suppose for refueling—the gray-white tip of Mt. Fuji could be seen in the distance. Though it was almost covered with a shroud of fog, the peak of the mountain broke in such a way as to suggest the mountain was wearing the fog as a ring. The Japanese on the base did not like the fact that I was taking pictures of their sacred mountain. Hence, no picture of Mt. Fuji!

Joe Perry

November 18, 1966

> *The world is a comedy to those who think*
> *and a tragedy to those who feel.*
> *—Horace Walpole*

I am back in the United States and settled.

Miscellaneous Thoughts

My philosophy of living is one of simple humanity. I do not wish to be great or rich or famous. Fame and fortune mean nothing to me. I have no great ambition for success as the word is interpreted today. I want only to live as simply and humanely as possible.

> I'm just a country boy—
> Money, money have I none.
> But I have silver, silver in the stars,
> And gold in the morning sun,
> And gold in the morning sun.
>
> —George McCurdy

I want to be able to look back on my life and say, "It was a good, full, and productive life. What successes I achieved were not at the expense of others. I didn't use anyone as a stepping-stone. I hurt no one. I killed no one. I loved and was loved. I had no hate for anyone nor did anyone for me. I was a good husband and father. Never did I get too far away from the beauty and majesty of nature.

Dr. Schweitzer said, "Just do what you can. It's not enough merely to exist. It's not enough to say 'I'm earning enough to support my family. I do my work well. I'm a good father. I'm a good husband.' That's all very well. But you must do something more. Seek always to do some good, somewhere. Every man has to seek his own way to make his own self more noble and to realize his own true worth. You must give of time and love to your fellow man. Even if it's a little thing, do something for those who have need of help, something for which you get no pay but the privilege of doing it. Remember you don't live in a world all your own. Your brothers are here too."

These past two paragraphs were submitted to *Reflections* (Dallas Baptist College) in February 1971 and published in April.

February 7, 1967

1. Answer John Vinson's letter.
2. Valentine cards.
3. Work on short story hobby.

April 1, 1967

I am on the road again—this time in San Antonio and parts unknown. Tomorrow morning, I leave Kelly AFB at ten—destination unknown. If I'm going anywhere other than back to Washington, it's a good thing I brought my checkbook along—though it really won't help much.

The Boss is extending some Texas hospitality to approximately forty Latin American ambassadors and their wives in preparation for the South American conference in two weeks—maybe I'll end up in South America. Who knows?

Sondra was with me most of today, and we had a tremendous and inexpensive time. We strolled along the banks of the San Antonio River during the diplomatic river parade.

I will have to pack after I get off duty in the morning. I won't have much time for anyone or anything. I must sleep in the communications center again tonight. I haven't even slept in my room on this trip. Oh, well. *C'est la vie!*

Trick Three Escapades

April 16, 1967

I've worked on all three tricks (work groups), and trick three is by far the best. Lately there has been too much cutting up on duty, but we always get the job done before any other activities occur. We're really a close-working and associating group, but CG is the one exception. After duty on Friday night, we went to Rick Hodge's place for a little party. There were six of us in all: Rick, Ed Neumann, John Tiffin (The Pillsbury Doughboy), Nat Jones (trick chief), Doug Ludvigsen (Rick's roommate), and me.

I never would have thought I'd be enjoying a picnic—on a rooftop—at two o'clock in the morning, but we all walked upstairs to the third floor and climbed up the ladder onto the roof. The other guys drank beer and ate chips and dips. I just stuck to cokes and potato chips. It was a strange, free-feeling sensation to do something on the spur of the moment. It was fun even to a person with vertigo. We ended our party at four because we all had to be back on duty Saturday evening.

Mo, "Cheap Petty" (Sharkus), and Ski (Ted G.) are all on TDY as well as Burnham. Soon they'll be back though, and things will be back to near normal, which is normal for us.

I am looking forward to my marriage (two more months), my future in the agency (two more years), becoming a father (soon, but not prematurely), finishing school, and becoming a teacher or preacher—probably a teacher. Rick says I should be in the cloth (ministry). He doesn't know I am licensed as a preacher, and it is just as well. Somehow, it seems so hypocritical. Sleepiness is taking my coherence, so I must discontinue these written thoughts while I alleviate the situation.

May 27–31, 1967

The most eventful part of our short ranch trip was the stopover in Newport News, Virginia. We did not see the christening of the *Kennedy*, however. We had to stay on the plane. The apartments above the Johnson City Bank were very nice and inexpensive.

Arab-Israeli War

May 27–31, 1967

War between Arabs and Israelis has started in the Middle East. On May 22, Egypt's President Nasser closed the Gulf of Aqaba to all Israeli ships. This in itself was an act of war as the Gulf of Aqaba is an international waterway, which under a 1957 treaty is supposed to be open to all countries. Israel, seeing this as a threat to them, mobilized its forces while yielding to a US plea for diplomatic attempts to reopen the gulf. For a few days prior to June 5, Arabs in countries with Israeli borders were proclaiming a quick demise of Israel in the impending holy war (jihad).

After the breakout of hostilities on Monday, Secretary General U Thant of the UN said his initial report indicated the outbreak was provoked by Egyptian and other Arab troop advances into or on the borders of Israel.

It is now June 7 (late evening), and the Israeli military successes have been incredible. The Egyptians would be wise to agree to a UN cease-fire before they find themselves confronted with the threat of complete and total defeat. Nasser bit off a bit of hickory, and it is now beginning to swallow him.

June 9, 1967

War continues, though Israel, Egypt, Jordan, and Syria all have agreed to a cease-fire. Fighting today was in Syria and along Israeli borders (according to Gideon Rafael, the Israeli UN representative). Israel has taken Bethlehem, Jerusalem, Jericho, and it will be quite difficult for anyone to persuade her to give them up when and if peace talks start.

Moshe Dayan said, "Israel will never again lose Jerusalem." Dayan is defense minister and described as a "one-eyed Israeli hero." He was a hero in 1956 and probably is again now.

While there is war in the Middle East, I am waiting for a plane home at the Andrews passenger terminal. A guy can learn a lot about the subconscious habits of others when he observes them while spending the night in an air force passenger terminal.

A3C Lapsley chews the tips of his fingernails while watching TV in a state of boredom. He uses his forefinger to rub just below his nose as though he were trying to keep himself from sneezing. He has a neat personal appearance. He must be the kind of person worth knowing. His glasses hide what appear to be warm, brown eyes.

June 10, 1967

At 0615, I'm still waiting for a possible seat on a plane to Dallas. There's a plane leaving at 0700. The vehicle has three seats available. Twelve people are waiting for transportation to San Antonio or Dallas, and the odds aren't too good. Some have been waiting longer than I have.

Staff Sergeant Bergholz—a pale, bespectacled, semi-intellectual type—has the appearance of a world traveler. I doubt he has been anywhere except Omaha, Washington, and New York. He often strikes an arms-folded, all-omnipotent pose. Light rimmed glasses blend with a pale face to make him look rather pasty. I pity him because he is so incomplete. What makes me such an expert? Nothing. I have just developed the habit of observing people.

Rogers—the mousy type—often sits with hand under chin. Has a small face with deep-set, beady eyes. He talks in a high, squeaky voice. He is rather small and thin—almost slinky. He sleeps with both legs folded up. Harmless!

Perry must be some kind of nut! He subconsciously notes the habits of other people and records them in writing.

I am going home alone, but when I return, I will no longer exist as a single person! Sondra and I are getting married

June 16, 1967

I am a little apprehensive about the changeover from single existence to a dual existence.

However, I'm not worried about our marriage. Sondra and I love each other completely. Of course, we have not yet experienced the sexual aspects of love. We'll save that for June 16th and thereafter.

Marriage

June 17, 1967

We were married yesterday. Who has time now to write in a journal?

June 19, 1967

My birthday, but I am still planning to leave tomorrow for West Virginia and Washington. It will be a pleasant, if somewhat unusual, honeymoon. I know it will be hard for Sondra to become acclimated to being away from her parents. I'll try to make her happy, but at the same time, I will understand if she isn't exactly exuberant.

We will see some beautiful scenery together—scenes that God put here for our enjoyment and use. It is scenery that reminds one of steady and silent strength. I write, of course, of the mountains from which I came—the mountains through which we shall travel on our way to our new home—and our new life. It will be a happy one!

July 1, 1967

We left on Tuesday, and the trip started off on a rather heavy note. Sondra was a little pensive and quiet. I could tell she realized that each revolution of the wheels took her farther and farther from the home and family she so loved toward an uncertain future. Uncertainty is not an easy thing to confront. Yet she soon developed a positive attitude and began enjoying the trip and eagerly anticipated our future.

Confidentially, I too am enjoying the prospects of our future *together*—for we have a fulfilling and complete love. I emphasized the word *together* for a sensuous reason … the joining of male and female in a sensuous, sexual way. I guess I will have to delete these few sentences if I ever think this will be read by anyone else.

We had a good time at my grandparents' home in Madison. I wrote the following about my grandfather while we were there.

> Beside a swift-flowing Big Coal Stream,
> An old man
> Wears the hunter's uniform
> And remembers.
> His grandchildren smile when he speaks
> Of the soul
> Of the swiftly flowing stream.
> But he knows
> The vast, still beauty of the mountains
> And the joy

Of providing the necessities of life

The mountains call
And his body is strong
But today's world
Has no place for his experience and skill.
So he remembers
And his grandchildren all learn courage, honor,
And pride from his life.

July 4, 1967

After we had been in Madison for a night, I took Sondra
on a walk in the hills around the town. I thought I might
impress her with my memory from my childhood about the
layout of those hills. Those green hills were not exactly as
I remembered them, and we were lost, although I did not
share that fact with her.

She saw a brown bear about a hundred feet to our
right as we were descending a hill in the dense vegetation.
That "brown bear" turned out to be a brown tree stump.
Within a few minutes, we slid down a few yards of the hill,
stopping just before we would have run into some barbed
wire. I supposed the barbed wire was there to discourage
law enforcement officials from looking for stills that might
have been located nearby.

When we finally came to the bottom of one of the hills,
I realized we were on the other side of town. We had to
walk through downtown Madison in order to get back to
Mom and Dad Pauley's house at 212 Walnut Avenue.
The problem? Sondra had rolled her hair before we left

on this little expedition. We were perspiring profusely, and our clothes were grass- and dirt-stained from our tumble in the hills.

"Joseph," she said. "We can't go through town looking like this!"

"Why not?" I said. "It's either walk through town looking like this or go back through the hills. I can't guarantee we'll come out at the right spot above their house. Besides, it'll be quicker to go through town."

When we arrived back home, we quickly cleaned up and had a little visit with Mom and Dad Pauley. Of course, we had to wait for my grandmother to stop laughing. Dad Pauley kept himself fairly well composed.

When we arrived at their house the previous day, Mom Pauley said she had heard us coming because our tires were squealing. I had already checked the tires when we got out of the car. We had two bald tires, and two others were badly receding. The next morning before our mountain excursion, we had to buy two new tires and get the car correctly aligned.

It was during that visit that I first saw the stone with the words "Dad's Garden" carved in it. Because I always was a person of curiosity and always felt comfortable asking questions of them, I asked about the stone.

They replied, "You don't remember that story from when you were little? We're going to write it down for you. It'll take us a little while to write it, and we'll mail it to you."

I wonder about the curious way they acted. Are there things I need to know about the past? Should I be asking more questions? Mom explained that Dad Pauley felt he could write words that would explain things much better than he could say them.

I can still taste those fried apples and biscuits we had at the Pauley table.

Sondra Stories

I am reflecting on some things that have happened to Sondra in her brief time here. Shortly after we arrived at our apartment at Telegraph Hills in Alexandria, Virginia, she was somewhat amused. I had selected the apartment for what I thought was a sensible strategic reason: it was only about fifty feet from the outside basketball courts.

The front door was decorated, in lieu of curtains or blinds, with a six-foot poster of Clint Eastwood as he appears in the movie *A Fistful of Dollars.* We have discovered small kids like to look below the poster, I suppose, to see what type of people live behind that poster. The door is mostly glass, and I found this an inexpensive way to temporarily decorate and keep out the sun.

We have a curious neighbor who likes to crack open her door in the morning just as I am leaving for duty. One morning, I asked Sondra as I was leaving, "Hey, when are we going to get married anyway?"

The door was quickly closed, and we never had that problem again.

45

I had to take Sondra over to the basement of the Pentagon for her military ID photo. This would allow her entrance to the military base to buy groceries and other necessities at lower prices than she could get at public stores. Sondra didn't like the looks of the picture, and she requested a different pose. They allowed her to have several different poses—and she got to choose the one she wanted. Would they have allowed me to do that? Perish the thought!

August 23, 1967

Shortly after we set up housekeeping (with one twin bed, a big green desk, and my air force foot locker serving as a coffee table), it was necessary for Sondra to drive me to The Shop (secret location) from which I would be taken to Andrews Air Force Base with anyone else who was going on the trip. I later learned she had gotten lost on the way back to the apartment and had ended up in Maryland because she had been in the wrong lane on the freeway. She stopped the car on the freeway and got out of the car crying. A kind motorist stopped, and when he understood the problem, he gave her directions back to Alexandria. It must have been exasperating for her!

On a different occasion, I was on call. If a trip came up unexpectedly, I must already have a bag packed and be ready to go with as little as two hours' notice. When the call came to our apartment, I wasn't home from my shift yet.

Sondra asked the caller to repeat himself because she had orange juice cans in her ears and couldn't understand him. I had a difficult time explaining that when I got to The Shop. "Hey, Perry, what's it like to have a wife who wears orange juice cans in her ears?" Ladies often wear little orange juice cans as rollers for their hair. They just don't talk with people in the White House about such things.

I find myself getting quite involved with some of the people who live here in and near the Telegraph Hill Apartment Complex. Charlie ("Slick") Underwood and Curtis Thomas are like younger brothers to me. Naturally, they can't take Freddy's place, but he is back in Dallas, and I don't see him every day.

Charlie is a good-natured, well-liked, funny, lonely guy! His parents are threatening to send him to military school because he does get into some mischief. However, I think that is the worst thing they could do. You don't draw your kid closer to you by sending him away. Charlie is somewhat a "blithe spirit" and is too valuable a person to be tampered with. My respect and admiration for Richard Paton, Larry Dietz, and John Paton is something I can't adequately put into words. I can only feel it. I am honored to have them as younger friends. I coach them on a volunteer basketball team. We don't have a good record, but we do have a good time.

Doug and Rich are the indomitable duo. They're lively and not half as bad as they try to make themselves appear.

Joe Perry

October 1967

Last week, I returned from a presidential trip. As we were taxiing on the runway (tarmac) after landing at Andrews, we received an urgent message from the control tower: *There is an automobile coming toward the plane. Please be in lockdown.*

"Lord, please don't let it be a 1967 white Chevrolet Impala," I quietly prayed.

As the Secret Service agents on the plane were getting ready to combat this intrusion, the announcement was made: *There is a white 1967 Chevrolet Impala on the tarmac, and the auto has been stopped. Proceed with caution.*

I had visions of being immediately transferred to Thule, Greenland, because it was Sondra and our car on the tarmac. I was allowed to deplane after explaining how I thought it was my car and my wife.

"What are you doing?" I asked in what I thought was a very calm manner.

"I just wanted to see the plane," she said.

I wasn't shipped off to Greenland, but I did learn that two security personnel from Andrews were immediately reassigned. Security was supposed to be very tight. I suspect those airmen were tight in a different way.

December 1967

A wonderful lesson I have been taught by a thirteen-year-old boy during the Lottie Moon offering emphasis at the Downtown Baptist Church of Alexandria, Virginia.

Somehow I became the royal ambassador leader for our church's boys group. For our Lottie Moon emphasis, I challenged our boys to work or do extra chores to earn money to contribute to the Lottie Moon Christmas offering for foreign missions. "I will match what you give from your earnings—dollar for dollar," I said, anticipating that my boys would earn about fifteen dollars.

Jimmy Johnson and his younger brother, Bobby, took a wagon around their neighborhood and collected newspapers to sell. The rate was about one dollar per hundred pounds of newspapers. When I heard what these boys were doing, I was astonished. The boys earned fifty dollars from their newspaper collecting. Do you realize how many pounds of newspapers that is at one dollar per hundred pounds? That's five thousand pounds of old newspapers.

Jimmy has a condition where one of the bones in his leg hasn't grown enough to keep up with the rest of his body. Jimmy has had to use crutches for several months, and he will have to use them until the bone growth catches up. These boys taught me that a person is limited only by what he thinks are his limitations.

Assassinations

November 1963

President JFK assassinated

April 1968

Martin Luther King assassinated

June 5, 1968

Robert Kennedy assassinated. I tried to write about this senseless violence, but I couldn't.

July 1968

Where does it end? How many roads must a man walk down before he pays attention to the street signs of violence? When I was a young boy one of the places where we briefly lived was a duplex on Peabody Avenue in Dallas. Living in the other part of the duplex was officer J.D. Tippitt, and his wife. He was the police officer killed by

Lee Harvey Oswald on the same day as Oswald allegedly killed President Kennedy.

I have waited a month before trying to write anything about RFK because I didn't want to confuse emotion with opinion. I have, however, done just that. For now, I can write nothing.

I only know that we saw Robert Kennedy in April on a campaign stop in little Madison, West Virginia. He was an impressive speaker. Sondra stood on the base of a lamp pole in order to take a picture of him speaking on the courthouse steps. My grandmother, who had vowed she certainly wouldn't make any special effort to go see a politician, did anyway.

Kennedy was campaigning for the Democratic nomination for president. He actually started campaigning before Johnson announced that he wouldn't seek reelection. Hubert Humphrey is also running for the nomination. Vice President Humphrey has sent us an autographed picture of himself. I also have a picture of John F. Kennedy and several others of the President in 1968 White House scenes. We shall treasure them and preserve them for future generations of Perry descendants.

There are certain events I want to preserve for my future children and grandchildren that need clarity I am not sure I can preserve. But I must try.

One assassination in a country is one too many. There are two that occurred in 1968 in the United States. On the evening of April 4, 1968, Martin Luther King Jr. spoke to a group in Memphis, Tennessee. In his speech that evening he said, "I have been to the mountaintop, and I have seen into the Promised Land. I may not get there with you, but 'mine eyes have seen the glory of the coming of the Lord. He is tramping out the vintage where the grapes of wrath are stored. He hath loosed the fateful lightning of his terrible swift sword; his truth is marching on.'"

On Friday, April 5, 1968, Dr. King was shot while he stood on the balcony on the third floor of a Memphis motel in front of the room that had come to be known as the "Abernathy-King Room." When the news was broadcast, I knew there would be trouble. I just didn't know how much. In Washington and other cities around the country, there were riots, burning buildings, lootings, and violence on a wide scale.

On Saturday, April 6, my car had been parked on the Ellipse behind the White House while I was at work. Even though there was violence only a few blocks away, it was thought that it would not touch that area of the city. A machine gun nest had been set up at the Capitol. That, however, was more than a few blocks away. Two of the tires on my car had been slashed. I went back into the basement of the White House to use the phone and inquire if I could buy two tires on credit. Money was an object with which I had very little familiarity, especially enough to buy two new tires. A supervisor made a phone call, and sent me to the White House garage (secret location). I was given two tires that had been ordered for the presidential limousine. However, the wrong-sized tires had been delivered, and they were useless as far as the limousine was concerned. They were the right size tires for my car, however. Only two people know our car has presidential tires, and we're not talking.

Two days later, while I was walking through a cemetery in Alexandria, I saw a black family who appeared to be camping there. As I discovered, they had been burned out in DC, his store had been burned, and they were living in the cemetery.

The man who was head of the family said, "It's better for us to live here with what little we have left than to die out there."

Though they appreciated my sincere offer, they would not come home with me. He had been burned out by irrational black people, and he wondered what would happen to all of us if they went home with a white man. We prayed together, and when I stopped by to leave a little food the next day, they were no longer there.

The sixties are, indeed, hazardous times.

January 13, 1969

I am out of the air force as of the last of October 1968 (early release). Sondra and I will be moving to Dallas after Richard Nixon is inaugurated. I don't have much confidence that Nixon is what our nation really needs at this time, and I hope I am wrong.

Johnson was a strong president during difficult times. He accomplished civil rights legislation that perhaps could not have been legislated under another president. Vietnam and the accompanying protests (some of which Sondra went to see with her friend, Linda, from next door) have sapped his strength. His retirement won't be a lengthy one, I predict. His health will continue to deteriorate, and his heart will probably give out.

A famous Englishman, Horace Walpole, once said, "Life is a comedy to those who think—a tragedy to those who feel." I cannot yet determine whether I am a feeling thinker or a thinking feeler.

I must come to the conclusion though that today's depressed generation is made up of paralyzed feelers. They look at what they consider to be the sad state of the world today (crime, war, apathy by the older generation), and without thinking, they add to that sad state of affairs by drowning themselves in the clutches of drugs. So, while I understand reasons for the revolution or rebellion, I can't go along with those who need the crutches of drugs in order to avoid coping with the problems of today's world. Today's problems were caused by those who couldn't get along without a crutch.

Ray, the Spider, and the Ant

In August 1969, Sondra and I took a memorable trip through the Southland to visit our Alexandria friends. The homesickness was almost unbearable. Before we left Alexandria this time, we even went apartment hunting because we had decided to move back to Alexandria. Our friends—the Wrights, Frantzes, Hoerdegens, Bowens, Paulsens, Johnsons, and others—made us feel so welcome.

On the way back to Dallas, we stopped for a couple of days in Madison, West Virginia. Ray came that far with us. It was an enjoyable time for the three of us. Ray and I spent some time walking through the mountains together. We became particularly fascinated by a classic battle between a spider and a black ant that was caught up in the spider's web. We must have spent an hour watching their various maneuvers. How does the sting or bite of an ant affect a spider? The ant finally had the sting taken out of his attack by the spider's continued weaving and smothering. When we left the scene, the ant was quite immobile.

Ray and I talked quite a bit during the visit both among ourselves and with Sondra and my grandfather. I will always remember that trip. My grandfather (Dad Pauley) said nothing about it, but I was reminded of an incident that occurred when I was about five years old. I had found a cocoon, and it was apparent that the resident of that cocoon was having a difficult time getting out. When I helped it open the cocoon, the butterfly died! I was overcome with grief for that little thing, and I asked Dad Pauley why it had died.

"Joey," he said, "when that butterfly was struggling to get out of the cocoon, it was building strength to live once it was free from the cocoon. When you helped it, it didn't have enough strength to live."

"You mean I killed it when I tried to help it?" I cried.

"Yes," he said. "You have a tender heart and you wanted to help a creature in distress, but that creature needed the distress so he could build up enough strength to be able to fly great distances in his life."

In my life, I have learned that humans also may encounter difficulties that will strengthen them for more strenuous times to come. My grandfather taught me a lot, yet I sometimes had the feeling there was so much more he wanted to teach me even when Ray and I shared our fascination with the struggles of the ant and spider.

January 1, 1971

Except for an August entry in 1969, two years have passed since my last entry in this journal. Were they so uneventful as to warrant no mention? No. But the combination of school, work, and being a husband has left no time for recording events and thoughts.

I took some correspondence course work from a military-connected university while I was in the White House Communications Agency of the DCOU (Defense Communications Operations Unit), and I have been a student at North Texas State University since the latter part of January 1969. The classes have been difficult because I have also been working full-time at the Dallas Police Department and commuting to Denton during the week. Four or five hours a night is about how much sleep I get after studying or doing homework. My GPA has suffered, and it is now just above a 2.0. I am thinking of transferring to Dallas Baptist College, which is just a ten-minute drive from home.

My work in the records section of the Dallas Police Department includes filing police reports of crimes against persons and crimes against property and making copies of accident reports for people who have been involved in vehicle accidents. It's not too difficult, but it is a full-time job and helps put bread on the table. The GI Bill helps a great deal in funding my schoolwork. Sondra teaches school, and together, we are earning enough to make a living.

In addition to school and work, I need to make sure that Sondra and I have quality time to keep growing together. In addition to working as a teacher, Sondra is our church and youth choir pianist at Bethany Baptist in Pleasant Grove.

After our New Year's celebration with Doug and Sherry, I feel inspired and compelled to write about two of the most important people in our lives.

Sondra and I have discovered in our growing love relationship that it is not exclusive. In fact, as paradoxical as it seems, the more we love each other, the more room there seems to be for loving others. There should be various English words that communicate the different types or ways of loving people. However, my vocabulary hasn't discovered these various words. We love each other emotionally, physically, sexually, and mentally. We are committed to each other. We also love her parents in an emotional and mental way. We love my mother, brother, and sisters. But each love is different. Is it because we love each other so much that we are able to love others so much? Is it the love of God for us that creates love in our hearts for others?

How do I put that *love* into words? How do I describe it? It is permanent. Our love for Doug and Sherry is, I suppose, the type of love a godparent would feel. So, are there no problems with this?

A problem has arisen. Doug has a problem that causes him to be moody. He has a crush on Sondra. Writing the word *crush* seems to trivialize his feelings, and I don't mean to do that. I must help him deal with the confusion that comes from an adolescent boy dealing with feelings for an older woman. I can't solve the problem by writing about it in a journal. So, I shall just be patient, understanding, supportive, hopeful, and prayerful. In the meantime, I would like to express myself on a variety of subjects.

A man is killed in Vietnam
I feel the bullets in my shattered head.
A child is crying in his heart.
His tears could be my own.
I know that animals help man
When slaughtered in a test tube lab,
But dead dogs and squirrels in the roadway
Are in my minds crematorium for days.
I find it hard to understand why someone takes my
words from me and sells them to the world as though
they were his own.
A friend?
Once upon a time he was
But then he stole my "Time of Noon"
And my "Lonely People"
And my ideas as well.
Another might not come by soon.

I had a pet dog
Who took my underwear once
But only to another room.

There is war, and I feel another's death!
There are tears, and I feel another's pain!
There is fire, and I feel burned!
There is chilly cold, and I feel numbed!
There is Sondra's love for me
And my love for her
And the love we both feel for the special ones
That keeps us warm and very much alive!

March 7, 1971

Yesterday the morning crept in like a young colt unsure of itself. A soft and almost imperceptible breeze seemed to slowly push the darkness of night away and make room for the day. The two of us were in bed. Sondra was still in a peaceful sleep, and I was waiting for the breeze to finish its job.

The alarm clock was poised and waiting to put its official seal of approval on the proceedings by awakening the household just as it does at seven every morning. But this wasn't just another morning. It was a morning and a day that we were going to share with people whom we really love. I anticipated the joy that was to be ours on this day.

When I could stay there no longer, I rose from bed, went to the window of our upstairs bedroom on Barberry Street, pulled the blinds, and looked out upon a rising sun playing hide and seek with the clouds and the tops of the tall trees. Morning had arrived. I was expecting a great day.

My first thought was to turn off the alarm and let Sondra sleep until 7:30. She could be fixing breakfast while I went to pick up Doug and Sherry. At least, that was our original plan.

April 16, 1971

That Saturday was a great day of fun. It was almost as though we had a ready-made family for a day. Of course, Sondra and I are a family—but Doug and Sherry are just like a part of us. Perhaps I am guilty of covetousness. Love can sometimes be painful, confusing, and complicated.

Doug thinks I am jealous of him because Sondra has a good time with them on Friday nights. So does Sondra sometimes! Until yesterday, I hadn't been able to successfully communicate my fear to her. Fear? Yes. Fear causes me to act a little strange. How do I explain my fear of heredity? I can't! I can only feel the fear that comes over me when I begin to doubt myself—when I begin to think that I will make people unhappy just as he did, that I'll cause my wife to dislike me just as he did his wife. He bred a history of marriage failure. He has been married three times—all to the same woman, my mother. She has been married five times.

I don't really know how many times my older brother, Lewis Gene Bradley, has been married. My older sister has been married and divorced twice. My younger sister has been married twice. Is my family capable of having happy marriages? Is there a hereditary gene in us that is destructive? The love that Sondra and I have cannot be destroyed by anything or anyone except ourselves— except me and my self-doubt and fear. This fear is what I feel—not jealousy of Doug. How do I convince him of that? God grant me the wisdom I need so much!

One of Doug's favorite songs is "Bridge over Troubled Waters" by Simon and Garfunkel. I want to be a bridge for him. Lord, make us a bridge over his troubled waters as we depend upon you to be a bridge over ours.

April 1971: Victims or Victors?

April 18, 1971

If we live under a handicap—and who doesn't—let us not pity ourselves. The tragedy is not to be found in the handicap but in our inability to live within the margins of our strength. For even within our limitations, there is an opportunity to improve and find contentment. We should rejoice with what we have—and not be dissatisfied with what we don't. The secret of rising above rather than being limited by our handicaps—of being victors instead of the victims of circumstances—is to be found not in rebellion but in adapting and making the most of situations that confront us.

April 19, 1971

Now is really a great time to be alive. Discoveries that have taken place within our lifetimes are both wonderful and terrifying. The possibilities of what man can yet do seem unlimited, but the value of any new discoveries will depend upon how they are used—for destructive or constructive purposes, to hurt or to heal, to hinder or to help. How we respond will depend upon how strong within us is the desire to serve, upon whether or not our love for others is greater than our fear of others, upon the extent we are willing to sacrifice and place service above self, upon how much we are willing to give for the sake of the welfare of all. The extent to which we are committed to ideals will determine the use we make of power; ultimately, the spiritual will control the material.

May 23, 1971

Lethargy has set in upon me. Tomorrow I have two exams (Spanish and English), and I just can't push myself to study anymore! This will be the final day of school for the term, and it can't end too soon for me. I am really tired.

I have also decided to resign my teaching position in Sunday school at Bethany Baptist. I was not doing the job well enough. There could have been many reasons for the failure, and I really don't know for sure what the actual reasons are. I worked hard at trying to show my class that they should love one another. That was my primary goal. I believe that life is empty darkness except when there is urge, and all urge is blind except when there is knowledge, and all knowledge is vain except when there is work, and all work is empty except when there is love; and when you work and love, you bind yourself to yourself, and to one another, and especially to God.

May 29, 1971

Trust Me

You said, "I'll always be there"
And you are.
Sometimes the distance that you keep
Is as difficult for me to bear
As is the proximity
Of anyone I don't care for.
Trust me
Even if to make you happy
Means to leave you to yourself.

Trust Me (2)

I said, "I'll always be there."
And I am.
But sometimes the distance that you keep
Is as difficult for me to bear
As the proximity of anyone I don't care for.

Trust me and I'll do good things for you
Even if to make you happy
Means to leave you to yourself.

May 30, 1971

The Searchers is a writing born in my heart, born in the pain of ending one life and beginning another, born in the excitement of the continuing search for life's meaning.

Some people do not have to search; they find their niches early in life and rest there, seemingly contented and resigned. They do not seem to ask much of life or even take it seriously. At times, I envy them, but usually I do not understand them. Seldom do they understand me.

I am one of the searchers. There are, I believe, still a few of us. We are not unhappy, but we are not really content. People live in one of two kinds of tents: *con*tent or *discon*tent. We searchers are in some discontent, and we continue to explore life, hoping to recover its ultimate secret. We continue to explore ourselves, hoping to understand. We like to walk along the beach. We are drawn by the ocean, taken by its power, its unceasing motion, its mystery, and its unspeakable beauty. We like forests and mountains, deserts and hidden rivers, and the lonely cities as well. Our sadness is as much a part of our lives as our laughter is. To share our sadness with one we love is perhaps as great a joy as we can know—unless it is sharing our laughter.

We searchers are ambitious only for life itself, for everything it can provide. Most of all, we want to love and be loved. We want to live in a relationship that will not impede our wondering, prevent our search, or lock us inside prison walls. It will take us for what little we have to give. We do not want to prove ourselves to another or compete for love.

This is written for wanderers, dreamers, and lovers— and for lonely men and women who dare to ask of life everything good and beautiful. It is for those who are too gentle to live among wolves.

Poetry and Prose

The following poems and prose writings were written or composed over the past few years on various pieces of paper, envelopes, napkins, or whatever was available. They appear in the order in which they were written (after *Lonely Voices*) but are not dated.

Too Gentle to Live Among Wolves

There are men too gentle to live among wolves
Who prey upon them with IBM eyes
And sell their hearts and guts for martinis at noon.

There are men too gentle for a savage world
Who dream instead of snow and children
And wonder if the leaves will change color soon.

There are men too gentle to live among wolves
Who anoint them for burial with greedy claws
And murder them for a merchant's profit and gain.

There are men too gentle for a corporate world,
Who dream instead of candied apples, Ferris
wheels
And pause to hear the distant whistle of a train.
There are men too gentle to live among wolves
Who devour them with eager appetite and
search for
Other men to prey upon and suck their
childhood dry.

There are men too gentle for an accountant's world
Who dream instead of Easter eggs and fragrant
grass
And search for beauty in the mystery of the sky.

There are men too gentle to live among wolves
Who toss them like a lost and wounded Dove.
Such gentle men are lonely in a merchant's world,
Unless they have a gentle one to love.

Little Boy

Little boy, I miss you, with your sudden smile
And your ignorance of pain.
You walked into my life and devoured it—without
Anything but misty goals to keep you company.

Your heart beat mightily when I chased you
And thus captured, you were a great prize—
The captured who captured the capturer.

When did you lose your eyes and ears?
When did taste buds cease to tremble?
Whence this sullenness, this mounting fear,
This quarrel with life—
Demanding understanding or meaning?
The maddening search is leisure's bonus—
The pain that forbids you to be a boy!

My Easy God Is Gone

My easy God is gone—the one whose name
I knew since childhood.
I knew his temper, his sullen outrage,
His ritual forgiveness.
I knew the strength of his arm,
The sound of his insistent voice.
His beard bristling, his lips full and red
With moisture at the mustache,
His eyes clear and piercing,
Too blue to understand all
His face too unwrinkled to feel my child's pain.
He was a good God—so he told me—
A long-suffering and manageable one.

I knelt at his feet and kissed them,
I felt the smooth countenance
Of his forgiveness.
I never told him how he frightened me,
How he followed me as a child
When I played with friends or trick-or-treated

For candy on Halloween.
He was a predictable God,
I was the unpredictable one.
He was unchanging, omnipotent, all-seeing,
I was humorous and helpless.

He taught me to thank him for the concern
Which gave me no chance to breathe,
For the love which demanded only love in return—
And obedience.
He made pain sensible and patience possible
And the future foreseeable
(I would always be moving, changing schools,
Dealing with school bullies who saw
The new kid as a challenge to their position).
He, the mysterious, took all mystery away,
Corroded my imagination,
Controlled the stars and would not let
them speak for themselves.

No, my easy God is gone—he knew
Too much to be real,
He talked too much to listen,
He knew my words before I spoke.
But I knew his answers as well—
Computerized and turned to dogma.
His stamp was on my soul,
His law locked cross-like on my heart,
His imperatives tattooed on my breast,
His aloofness canonized in ritual.

Joe Perry

Now he is gone—my easy, stuffy God—God
Who offered love bought by an infant's fear.
Now the world is mine with all its pain and warmth,
With its' every color and sound.

A dog barks, and I weep to be alive,
A cat studies me, and my joy is boundless.
I lie on the grass and boy-like, search the sky.
The clouds turn to angels,
The winds whisper of heaven for me.

Oh, yes, my easy God is gone now,
Replaced by one who is real,
One whom I understand better.
Maybe I was the easy one who placed
Him in all those niches.

I have another god now.
I have beauty and joy and transcending loneliness,
I have the beginning of love—as beautiful as it
Is feeble—as free as it is human.
I have the mountains that whisper secrets
Held before men could speak,
I have the ocean that belches life on
The beach and caresses it in the sand.

He is a friend who smiles when he sees me,
(And he always sees me),
Who weeps when he hears my pain,
I have a future full of surprises,

A present full of wonder.
I have no past—the steps have disappeared,
The wind has blown them away.

I stand in the heavens and on earth,
I feel the breeze in my hair.
I can shout to the North Star
And have it shout back,
I can feel the teeth of a headache,
The joy of laziness,
The flush of my own rudeness
(Though I am sorry for it)
The surge of my own ineptitude.
And I can know my own gentleness as well,
My wonder, my nobility,
I sense the call of creation, I feel its swelling,
I can lust and love, eat and drink,
Sleep and rise,
But my easy god is gone—and in his stead
Is the true god.
God of the Universe, my God,
Is the God of the mountains,
And the God of the valleys.

This poem was sent to an author/priest who, with a few minor changes, published it as his own. I wrote this to explain that God is so much more than what I thought of Him as a Child.

A Father Someday I'll Be

A father someday I'll be
Who whispers his love if but for a moment,
Who looks at a child and reverently gathers
Him in arms that all the ages ached for.
The desert days are torrid,
But the waters are sweet,
And there are palm trees
To challenge the sun's cruelness
Till shadows come at night to thrill the poet and
Rest the wanderer in the quiet coolness of peace
And passion linked in a woman's arms
Strong enough to hold a man's heart,
Gentle enough to touch the sadness in his face,
Wise enough to let him go apart
To dream and wander.

Word Dreams

I dream on words and lick them
And wonder
How old they are and who created them
When they were only grunts and groans?

Sometimes I'd rather grunt than talk
Because words belong to someone else.
My grunts are my own,
Lusty in my throat,
Strong in my chest,
Born in my belly.

Sometimes I'd rather scream than sing
Because I write the lyrics to my screams.

I dream on words and lick them
And wonder
Who created them
When they were only sobs and sighs
Of savages too proud to go to school
And learn how other men talk.

My sobs are my own,
Caught in my throat,
Heaving in my chest,
Aching in my belly.

Sometimes I'd rather weep than sing
Because I write the music for my tears.

Will you come tonight and listen to my symphony
Of grunts and groans and weeping?

I Saw My Face Today

I saw my face today
And it looked older,
Without the warmth of wisdom
Or the softness
Born of pain and waiting.
The dreams were gone from my eyes,

Hope lost in hollowness on my cheeks,
A finger of death pulling at my jaws.
So I murdered a golf ball
And wondered if I'd ever find you,
To see my face
With friendlier eyes than mine.

Freedom

Man does not want freedom.
He only talks of it,
Satisfied to choose his slavery
And to pay it homage.

Freedom asks too much;
Silence and strength,
The death of empty alliances,
An end to ego baths.
Freedom confronts loneliness
And lives with it,
Makes more of larks and lust,
Builds no monuments to itself.

Man does not want freedom,
He fears its demands
And only needs to talk of it—
The *free man* has no such need.

Man can live without freedom,
Content to laugh at slavery

And to know today
That yesterday's pain is gone.

Only I Will Know

Come tell me of your sadness
Where the forest flowers grow,
Where the whispering breeze
Binds the lips of the trees,
And only I will know.

Come tell me of your secret fears,
Where the beach is soft as snow
Where the sparkling spray
Binds the eyes of the day,
And only I will know.

Come tell me of your special dreams
Where the roaring rivers flow,
Where the white water blocks
All the ears of the rocks,
And only I will know.

Come tell me of your deepest joys
Where the desert winds still blow
Where the shifting of sand
Hides the face of the land,
And only I will know.

Come tell me of your fondest hopes
Where the mountains look below

Joe Perry

Where a gathering cloud
Cloaks the peaks in its shroud
And only I will know.

Come tell me all, my loved one,
As we saunter in the snow
Where the chill of the night
Robs the goblins of sight
And only I will know.

Come tell me all, my loved one,
When the land is wet with rain,
When the tears blind the eyes
Of the curious skies,
And only I will know.

Note: Whenever I send poems to publishers or authors, I use the pen name "Jessie Pearson." I shall stop that because I don't get credit for the poems.

Everything I Love Is Soft and Silent
(To my wife, Sondra)

Everything I love is soft and silent,
My dog, the morning, the end of day,
Even the moon in its way.

Everything I love is soft and silent,
The water, the forest, the snow at play,
Even the mountain in its way.

Everything I love is soft and silent,
The sun on the sand, a rainy day,
Even the wind in its way.

Everything I love is soft and silent,
The grass, the brook, the leaves at play,
Even you in your way.

June 1971

Tomorrow morning, our youth choir leaves on their mission trip to Galveston. They are a great group of young people who will not take much time for leisure at the beach. I hope they see it early in the morning before the onslaught of people ruins it for them. I can picture myself there on the beach in the early quiet of the morning. I wish I could be there with them. However, I will be with them spiritually, if not physically.

In two or three years, I will become a father. Who can believe it? I can, that's who! Over a year ago, in one of our infrequent family gatherings, my father, Ross Perry, said to me—within earshot of several family members, "I doubt you'll ever have any children!" The implication to me was quite clear: *I was not potent enough to cause a baby to be created.* His language wouldn't have been quite that polite.

I could have gotten angry because it did disturb me. However, I certainly didn't want him to know that. So, I just looked at him and left. *Why does he hate me so much?* I ask myself that time and time again. He was in the army stationed in Pittsburgh when I was born. The rest of the family lived with my grandparents, Mom and Dad Pauley, in Madison, West Virginia, when I was born. When I was older, I failed his "learn-to-swim" test several times. His method of teaching was to throw me into the river and expect me to follow his directions to relax, kick my legs, and use my hands to pull the water toward me. I nearly drowned three times, and he got very angry three times. I must have been a big disappointment to him, but that shouldn't have caused him to hate me.

Does he think I have a problem with sexual orientation? I'm not Gene, that's for sure. There is no need for me to prove anything to him or anyone else.

Quiet Mornings

I like the quiet mornings when the waves have washed the footprints from the shore,
when even the gulls are just beginning to stir,
and the heat of the day has not yet aroused the flies to search the seaweed for breakfast,
when the beach still has the sand of sleep in its eyes
and the driftwood looks like tired swimmers resting on the shore,
when the waves laugh at the rocks and playfully wash the night from their eyes.

Soon enough, the hungry gulls will dive for fish
And the waves will beat shape into the rocks.
Feet will pound on the beach,
And ladies will snatch the driftwood for lamps,
And I will face the day's demands,

Trampled like sand,
Wounded like the rocks,
Torn up like the wood,
Living for another quiet morning.

The Center of Your Soul

There is quiet water in the center of your soul where a
Son or daughter can be taught what no man knows.
There's a fragrant garden in the center of your soul
where the weak can harden, and a narrow mind can
grow.

There's a rolling river in the center of your soul,
An eternal giver with a rich and endless flow.
There's a land of muses in the center of your soul
Where the rich are losers and the poor are free to go.

So remain with me, then, to pursue another goal
And to find your freedom in the center of your soul.

Will You Be My Friend?

Who am I? I am not sure.
Once I was predictable. I was educated, trained, loved.

Not as I was but as I seemed to be. My role was my easy
way of hiding. There was no reason to change. I was
approved. I pleased. Then, almost suddenly, I changed.
Now I am less sure, more myself. My role has almost

disappeared. Friends aren't easy to find, and I dream a lot. Will you be my friend? Beyond roles.

Who am I? I am not sure.

I am more alone than before. Part animal, but not protected by his instincts or restricted by his vision. I am part spirit as well, yet scarcely free, limited by touch and time, yearning for all of life. There is no security. Security is sameness and fear, the postponing of life. Security is expectations and commitments and premature death. I live with uncertainty. There are mountains yet to climb, clouds to ride, stars to explore, and friends to find. I am all alone. There is only me—and I dream a lot. Will you be my friend? Beyond security.

Who am I? I am not sure.

I do not search in emptiness and need, but in increasing fullness and desire. Emptiness seeks any voice to fill a void, any face to dispel darkness. Emptiness brings crowds and shadows easy to replace. Fullness brings a friend, unique, implacable. I am not as empty as I was. There are the wind and the ocean, books and music, strength and joy within, and the night (though it can be lonely). Friendship is less a request than a celebration, less a ritual than a reality, less a need than a want. Friendship is you and me—and I dream a lot. Will you be my friend? Beyond need.

Who am I? I am not sure.

Who are you? I want to know. We didn't play ball together or hitchhike to school. We're not from the same town, the same part of the country, hardly the same world. There is no role to play, no security to provide, no commitment to make. I expect no answer save your presence, your eyes, yourself. Friendship is freedom, is flowing, and is rare. It does not need stimulation; it stimulates itself. It trusts, understands, grows, explores, smiles, and weeps. It does not exhaust or cling, expect or demand. It is—and that is enough—and it dreams a lot.

Will you be my friend?

There are so many reasons why you never should: I'm sometimes sullen, often shy, and acutely sensitive. My fear erupts as anger. I find it easy to give but difficult to receive. I talk about myself when I'm afraid and often spend a day with nothing to say.

But I will make you laugh and love you quite a bit,
And hold you when you're sad.
I cry a little almost every day
Because I'm more caring than the strangers ever know,
And if at times, I show my tender side
(The soft and warmer side I hide)
I wonder, Will you be my friend?

A friend
Who far beyond the feebleness of any vow or tie
Will touch the secret place where I am really I,
To know the pain of lips that quiver and eyes that weep,
Who will not run away when you find me in the street
Alone and lying mangled by my more than quota of defeats,
But will stop and stay—to tell me of another day
When I was beautiful?

Will you be my friend?
There are so many reasons why you never should:
Often I'm too serious,
Seldom predictably the same,
Sometimes appearing aloof and distant,
Probably I'll never change.
I falter often, abhor my frequent failures,
Speak love haltingly, yet try to show it often,
Have a karate brown belt, but never fight anymore.
But I will make you laugh
And love you quite a bit,
And be near when you're afraid.
I shake a little almost every day
Because I'm more frightened than the strangers ever
know,
And if at times I show my trembling side
(The anxious, fearful part I hide)
I wonder, Will you be my friend?
A friend who, when I fear your closeness,
Feels me push away,
And stubbornly will stay to share what's left on such
a day,
Who, when no one knows my name or calls me on
the phone,
When there's no concern for me—what I have or
haven't done—and those I've helped and counted on
have, oh so deftly run, who when there's nothing left
for me,
Stripped of charm and subtlety,
Will nonetheless remain.

Will you be my friend?
For no reason that I know
Except I want you so!

October 8, 1971

It has been a very strange and exciting week for me. I don't know how to explain it really to anyone, even Sondra. I have been possessed! Doubts about my planned teaching future have flooded my brain. I have stayed up late, planning to study, and ended up reading my Bible— and receiving from it an understanding that I must give myself over completely to God for his work. Now how can I logically explain that? I affirmatively answered what I thought was God's call to ministry when I was thirteen or fourteen, and later I repudiated it as being a self-inspired call. I wanted so much to be like my grandfather who was a preacher. Now I find myself losing track of time because I am completely immersed in whatever God is trying to show me. It doesn't even sound logical when I write it. So, how could I logically explain it to anyone? Something will have to happen soon.

Yesterday I talked with Phillip May, a new young friend at Dallas Baptist. He was very concerned and will pray for me. On Tuesday, I talked with Jack Ables and completely lost track of time. Today, I talked with Dr. Trammel and Dr. MacLeod. Both advised prayer, waiting, studying his Word, and meditating. This I will do. I am peacefully happy for the first time in months and don't even know why. One thing I have definitely concluded: God isn't bound by my sense of logic.

Jack Ables is a student at Dallas Baptist College, and he also works with me at the Dallas Police Department. Sometimes on lunch break, he and I will go to the men's restroom and play our adapted game of baseball. We take turns hitting and pitching. We make a ball by wadding up toilet paper and wrapping it in tape. If the ball is hit into the first stall it counts as a single; the second stall a double; the third is a triple; and the fourth (farthest away) is a homerun. Anything not hit into the stalls is an out. When there are three outs, we change sides. Anything hit into the commodes calls for a change of balls. We interrupt the game should men come in to use the facilities—*unless* they are drunk. We've had some high-scoring games in thirty minutes.

A Fleeting Vision

One day, for some reason known only to God
Who understands the motion of the planets,
The mystery of the stars,
There came suddenly and fleetingly to me
A burst of love so unlike any feeling I have ever known
That it grew like some mystic fire around my heart
And warmed the secret crevices where ego disappears.
I did not call it forth; it came.
Nor will I ever be the same,
Even if the vision never comes again.

I did not love at all—but rather, I was by love possessed.
And death joined life in a mysterious merging
As if my vast and loving letting go made some contact
With the motion of the universe,
As if some secret harmony hidden from me before
Was now as obvious as the wind, and each pulsing
Heart was but a feeble echo of some universal
beating—
Of man or animal or tempest. The heart of God!

Many things, all good, have happened to me since last I wrote. I have awakened from a long sleepwalk and found myself standing near the edge of a great danger. Thank you, God, for loving and wanting me.

Once a friend sent some of my poems to a publisher without my permission. He had expressed a desire to read them, and I, considering him to be a good friend, allowed him to read my private thoughts. One poem ended up in a religious song, and another under my pen name (Jessie Pearson) in a famous poet's poetry book. In a way, I am flattered, but no one else will be allowed to borrow my private writings.

Love and Breath Beyond Belief

Love and life and breath beyond belief
And dreams all destined to be fulfilled,
A heart too full to make sense,
With giraffes dancing with kangaroos
And songs lustier than a pumpkin moon,
With dancing stars and every moment making love

And bearing children too winsome to weep,
A hand long enough to reach the heavens
And to tickle them until they can only giggle
And shout delightedly:
"My God, it's beautiful! It's man!"

Matthew's Birth—His Poem

Wednesday, June 21, 1972

At two in the morning, Sondra woke me and said, "I think it's almost time."

Of course, I understood that to mean that the baby was coming. She had been very energetic on Tuesday, cleaning house like she hadn't in some time. I wasn't totally surprised. Her hospital bag was packed and sitting by the bedroom door. I was ready much quicker than she was, and she wanted to wash her hair before going. She didn't want any nurses or doctors seeing her hair looking less than its best.

Finally, we departed our house on Barberry Drive and left for Methodist Hospital. Preliminary examinations there determined that it would be a while yet. Sondra wanted me to go back home and get her hairdryer while she washed her hair again. When I came back, the nurses didn't like the idea of her using her hairdryer, but they liked the idea of her doctor seeing her with wet hair even less. While at home I picked up two volumes of my Keil-Delitzsch Hebrew commentaries, figuring I would have some time to use them during the day. Perish the thought. Though I tried, I just could not get into studying.

It was quite an eventful day. Sondra's parents came out, of course, but my mother didn't. There was a storm in early afternoon, and the hospital briefly lost power. They switched to their emergency power. Matthew Joseph Perry was born at 2:13 p.m., after a rather long labor. He had a shock of black hair and deep blue eyes.

Sondra was drowsy for a few hours. When I told her that my mother hadn't been able to come because a tree had fallen on her car and she was trapped inside, Sondra said, "That's nice."

I got a copy of that afternoon's *Dallas Times Herald* with the story about the huge storm and a lady in Oak Cliff trapped in her car on the front page, and we retained it for placement in his baby book. Matthew had all his fingers, toes, and other vital parts. So, we were very content. Statistics? He was seven pounds, eight ounces, and twenty-one inches long—normal in every way.

It's time for Mom and Dad to get some rest while we can. I have a feeling that our lives are undergoing a major change.

Matthew's birth made the day seem sunny and bright instead of cloudy and dark. Thank you, Lord! Our gift from God is here, and we'll do our best to raise him the way you want him raised.

January 2, 1974

I wonder what causes the well to run dry. Why are there short periods of productivity followed by long droughts? In the past, there have been periods when I couldn't write fast enough to record my thoughts. At other times, I can't seem to adequately write anything. A really good writer writes every day!

It's been more than eighteen months since I've written anything in my journal. Several times I started something only to later scratch it out or tear it out. Perhaps the things I would have written during those eighteen months were too painful to write about at that time. Even now, there is some suffering still.

FB Meyer, the famous English preacher of the last century, and his wife were especially fond of a young preacher. Once they went to hear him preach, and Mrs. Meyer came away from the service singing the praise of this great young preacher. She waxed eloquent in her praise of the young man until she noticed that Dr. Meyer was strangely silent. When she asked Dr. Meyer whether or not he thought the young man was a great preacher, he said, "He's good, but he'll have to suffer before he's ever a great preacher."

Later, after the young preacher had experienced the tragedy of losing a child in a drowning accident plus some financial difficulties, which I believe are inherent to the position of preacher, Dr. and Mrs. Meyer again went to hear the young man preach. Remembering her husband's reaction to hearing the young man the first time, Mrs.

Meyer was guarded in her comments about the young preacher. Finally, she asked Dr. Meyer his opinion of the young minister.

"Now," he replied, "he's a great preacher." Perhaps in his early ministry that young man was a larva in a cocoon, and having suffered in distress, he grew strong enough to become great.

How have I suffered? I suppose the mental anguish was the worst thing with which to cope. That Atkisson family affair was quite a distressing thing and it is still. Jerry actually got his rifle, pointed it at me, and ordered me to leave when I asked to see the marriage license. My mother and Jerry announced that they had gotten married in New Orleans. Originally I didn't question that. After all they were middle-aged adults who certainly had the right to do so. They didn't need anyone's approval. In fact, I hoped he could make her happy. But why wasn't there some evidence, some photographs, from the ceremony? My mother is a good woman, but she hasn't really made good choices concerning men.

The police department fiasco was quite painful. I know I was innocent of any wrongdoing, but I was put through so much that I began to feel persecuted. Accusations, questions, doubts, statements, suspension, appeal, and a lie detector test—at my request—resulted in my exoneration and reinstatement, but it was quite a hassle. After my reinstatement, I really had no desire to work for the police department anymore. I resigned—effective the same day as my suspension had been effective. No longer did I wish to be associated with the Dallas Police

Department. I probably should have just swallowed my pride and started back to work.

We were forced to sell our house prematurely. I found a night job, but it paid much less. Somehow I managed to stay in school. During the summer, I worked at an apartment complex mowing lawns, working to prepare apartments for occupancy, and doing any odd jobs necessary. Somehow, with the help of God, I managed to take eighteen hours of work in Summer school (clepping a few courses) and graduated on August 17.

On August 18, we moved to Fort Worth into seminary housing so that I could go to seminary. Neither of us had a job or promise of a job. There were people from University Baptist Church in seminary housing with the intent of helping us move in. By Sunday evening, I had a job as one of the church custodians. Sondra had an appointment to see about a teaching assignment that Monday morning.

Seminary Years

Seminary is really quite a different experience—much different from college in the attitude of students and in the quantity and quality of work expected from the students. I'm glad to be here. The police department, in their haste to find a scapegoat for some irregularities, nearly ruined my chance to enter seminary.

I remember my extreme anxiety and worry over the prospect of having the stigma of dishonor attached to my name. Had they succeeded, I could not have entered seminary—and could not have become a seminary-trained preacher. However, God handled things well, and I gained strength to endure hardship. He didn't always have my undivided attention; in truth, sometimes I wondered if he was going to work things through. My faith needed to be strengthened. Was I a larva in a cocoon having to be strengthened to survive?

The real culprit at work had been the person who pointed investigators in my direction. I thought it would be difficult to forgive that person, and it was, but I had to forgive if I was to have a closer relationship with my God.

January 3, 1974

We have been in Alexandria since December 28, visiting the Frantz family and other friends from our years of residence here. It has been a good week of visiting, talking, and fellowship. Was it necessary for me to return to Virginia before I could write anything again? Who knows? What other explanation is there? The Frantzes (mostly Ray) dressed Matthew in a Redskins outfit and took a picture for us.

February 25, 1974

Since November 3, 1973, Sondra and I have been working at Buckner Children's Home in Dallas as group parents— training to be house parents. It has been, and continues to be, a very educational experience. We were first assigned as group parents in Carnet, a dorm for teenage boys. Our experiences with those boys are detailed in a separate book entitled simply *Our Boys*.

March 5, 1974

On one of my rather frequent trips up the path of Huff Mountain to my favorite place, a boulder that juts out of the mountain and is big enough for me to lie on if I wanted, a resting place that provided a good view of the town of Madison, I found a rather plain-looking rock that was as black as coal. For some reason, I wanted immediately to keep that rock. When I reached my secluded spot, I turned that rock over and over in my hand until I had looked at it from almost every angle. Finally, the particular angle at which I held the rock in relation to the sun's rays produced a bright sparkle. To me, that rock became very valuable—more than a diamond that sparkles all over.

In some ways, our boys are like that black rock. I'm sure we'll see the sparkle in them if we keep looking from every imaginable angle. The sparkle of goodness is there.

April 17, 1974

We've been working in Crouch, a girl's dormitory, for two and a half months now. Consequently, we don't have the opportunity to look for those sparkles in the boys as we did earlier. We will, however, seize every available opportunity to help them sparkle or develop some spark of life. Our desire is to see them all won to Christ. He adds sparkle to the dullest things, even to me.

Working with teenage girls in Crouch is quite a bit more difficult for us than working with the boys in Carnett. These girls have never been subjected to much discipline before coming here. They, with some exceptions, tend to be loud, rowdy, and slouchy in dress and manners. Their low opinion of themselves is shared by many people on campus. Sometimes I think the administration finds all the girls they consider to be nearly hopeless and sends them to Crouch II (second floor of the dorm). These girls on the second floor of Crouch need much prayer, patience, and fair firmness from us. They can sparkle too if we look close enough.

Sondra, Matthew, and I have very little family time. On our day off each week, we usually leave campus and go to her parents' house. That gives them time with their grandson—and us a little time to be with family.

Note: Huff Mountain, written about earlier, did not really overlook Madison. It overlooked Mallory, a sawmill camp, near Oceana, West Virginia. I used author's license to move it to a different geographical location somewhat more familiar in my memories. I remember spending good times on that boulder.

November 28, 1974

I remember times in the not-too-distant past when Thanksgiving was a real time for family togetherness, a time when everyone in the family got together and enjoyed the company and presence of one another, a time when the inner spirits of the various members of the family were all of one accord. Today, as I tried to get my sister to talk to me, I wondered what has happened to those good old times. Perhaps it is not the times that have changed at all—perhaps the family has done all of the changing. Maybe it's me. How does it happen?

November 29, 1974

This past six weeks has been a kind of summary of life for me. Circumstances have brought me into close contact with what I may call the three great universal realities in life: birth, death, and memory.

I wrote a postcard to Ray about five weeks ago. In it, I promised to write him a long letter within a few days. I was very seriously tempted to add a tidbit of information on that postcard, a piece of news I knew Ray would be very interested in. However, I decided to withhold that information for a few days and include it in the long letter that I intended to write in just a few days. Circumstances have delayed the writing of that letter and altered the tone of the news I have to tell him.

Originally I planned to tell him that, barring "unforeseen complications," Matthew would have a baby brother or sister early next June. Now I must tell him that "unforeseen complications" did arise and "Christopher Michael" or "Rebecca" died an early death.

February 25, 1975

I have not actually written for some time now, and I have become like a closed seashell; if someone were to pick me up and hold me to their ear or eye, they would neither hear nor see anything. Not writing has made me dumb and mute. So, I have decided to make a conscious effort to write a little, if not in this journal, then in a scrapbook every day. I never want to be closed again.

February 26, 1975

Just Because

Just because it's today,
Just because a sun I never touched,

Touched me,
And a sky I couldn't hold,
Held me,
And a love I didn't understand,
Understood me.
Just because
The sun
And sky
And love
Are free,
I rejoice.

June 20, 1975

My Son
(To Matthew for tomorrow's third birthday)

God made a world out of his dreams,
Of magic mountains, oceans, streams,
Prairies and plains and wooded land,
Then paused ... and thought, *I need*
Someone to stand ...
On top of the mountains, to conquer the sea,
Explore the plains, and climb the trees.
Someone to start out small and grow,
Sturdy, strong, like a tree and so ...
He created you full of spirit and fun,
To explore and conquer, to romp and run,
With dirty face, banged-up chin,
With courageous heart and boyish grin.
When he had completed the task he'd begun,

He surely said,
"That's a job well done."

Our love for you, son, is deeper than any ocean,
As is God's, and greater than any need in your heart.
"Trust in the Lord with all your heart" (Proverbs 3:5–6).

Meredith's Beginnings—
Her Poem

October 7, 1975

Meredith Leigh Perry was born yesterday, Monday, October 6, 1975. Before I tell you about her birth, let me tell you about events leading up to her birth. Before her birth, we had a miscarriage. Though the baby was only three months along, we felt the loss most deeply. One of the girls at Crouch, when she was angry for whatever reason, shouted, "I hope you lose your baby." When we actually did, she was inconsolable. We questioned God until we were able to say, "We don't understand, but we love you and trust you and ask you to lead us in whatever way you want us to go."

The answer I seemed to get was Jeremiah 29:11. *"I know the plans I have for you," saith the Lord, "plans to prosper you ... and give you hope."* And, boy, did he give us hope!

I stayed home from the church at Ida this past weekend because Sondra and I were both thinking that the baby might be born anytime. I didn't want to be eighty miles away when Sondra's labor started. Saturday came, and one false alarm cropped up on Saturday night. Sunday was, beyond the shadow of a doubt, the longest day of the year. We left Matthew with his Morgan grandparents, thinking it would be easier for all concerned if we did that before we started for the hospital. Sondra was beginning to show some signs—I should say *feel* some signs—late Sunday night. We decided to stay awake and wait because the time was quite near.

At two o'clock on Monday morning, the time was as near as we wanted it to be. We went to Baylor Hospital. Sondra was examined, and we did some more waiting. Sondra was quite uncomfortable—and became increasingly more so. As it turned out, there was a simple explanation for her discomfort.

Unbeknownst to the nurses, Meredith Leigh Perry had decided it was time to make her appearance. At least, that's what I thought, and a quick examination by the nurse whom I summoned confirmed my opinion. By the time I returned from parking our car, Meredith Leigh had been born. I heard her before I saw her. I could talk with Sondra by telephone in the delivery room. I could hardly hear Sondra, but I had no trouble hearing the baby. She was berating the staff for trying to keep her waiting.

My first impression of Meredith was that she had a good set of lungs. She was born just before 4:30 a.m. Monday, October 6, 1975. Another blessing from God had arrived. God saw us through the heartbreak of miscarriage and brought us a beautiful baby girl. Great is the Lord and greatly to be praised always.

April 1976

Meredith gave us quite a scare last month. She appeared to be somewhat listless for a couple days. One morning, Sondra had Meredith and Matthew bundled up and ready to go to Nonnie's. Nonnie babysits the kids. When Meredith threw up some slimy green stuff, we decided Sondra would take Meredith to the doctor. I went on to seminary.

That morning, I received a message to call home immediately. When I did, Papa said, "Meredith has to have surgery right away—and you need to get to Children's now!" My VW and I made it from Southwestern in Fort Worth to Children's Medical Center in Dallas in twenty-five minutes, just in time for Meredith to go into surgery.

Sondra explained to me that Meredith had a rare condition called Meckel's diverticulum—a condition that occurs to maybe 2 percent of all babies. A stub of the umbilical cord wraps itself around the intestines and eventually causes a tear, causing intestinal contents to leak out. It was a very dangerous condition, but the surgeon operated immediately and corrected the problem. He had postponed a trip to El Paso to speak at a medical conference so he could do this unusual surgery.

Meredith was hospitalized for eleven days, and she did not like the tubes sticking in various parts of her body, including her feet. Several times, she pulled them out, and the medical staff patiently reinserted them. She got the finest care possible.

Since Matthew was not a recipient of a lot of attention for a couple weeks, Sondra took him to Kip's for a special breakfast.

June 19, 1976

It is my thirty-second birthday, and it is meaningless to me. I just have not been able to work up any enthusiasm whatsoever about celebrating my thirty-second birthday. It's not that I mind getting older—and at thirty-two, I still feel young and have no fear of advancing old age. The plain truth is there is no difference in this day and all the other days of the year.

Others have shown some excitement about my birthday. Sondra gave me a shirt and baked a chocolate cake. Her parents also gave me a shirt. Matthew sang "Happy Birthday" to us both (his birthday is Monday). All these things were pleasing—it's nice to be reminded that someone cares about you—but why not sometime other than my birthday? I suppose what's really bothering me is I haven't heard from my family.

Matthew's birthday on Monday is meaningful to me. On that day, we celebrate the fourth anniversary of the day God gave us a son. I haven't shown much appreciation for him lately—I really haven't been myself for a while—but I think I am returning to a state of mind somewhere near normal. Being a person of melancholy is sometimes a big drag.

June 21, 1976

It is the evening after a long and eventful day. For Matthew's fourth birthday, we gave him his presents early this morning. He received a play dump truck equipped with a bucket, a set of lawn tools (rake, hoe, and shovel) with a lawnmower (that makes mowing noises) so that he will have something to use when he helps his Papa work in the yard, and a Rangers T-shirt from us. He received the T-shirt at the baseball game on Friday night.

From his Morgan grandparents, he received a Fisher-Price play farm complete with stable, horses, saddles, and cowboys. In the evening, we had a picnic party at Kiest Park. Sondra made fried chicken, potato salad, and a cake. Carolyn, Jim, Jimmy, and Danny Bradley and Papa and Nonnie joined us for the picnic. It was a fun time for all.

Does Anybody Know Me?

January 11, 1977

I wrote this poem during the months of heartache. This poem was later published in *Best New Poets of 1986* under my own name.

Does anybody know me?
I am the person whom nobody knows—and I hurt inside.
Does anybody know me?
I am the person to whom everybody is nice—unbearably nice
But nobody really knows me—and I hurt inside.
Does anybody know me?
I am a person whom some people love,
But I can't let them really know me, and I hurt inside!
Does anybody know me?
I am a person who carries the American Express card,
But nobody really knows me, and I hurt inside.
Oh, I wish you knew me.
I wish you wanted to!
Then, I wouldn't hurt inside

July 6, 1977

I heard my grandfather preach at prayer service tonight in Madison Baptist Church. He is eighty-five years old and teaches better than many young preachers. He confided to me several days ago that it is becoming increasingly difficult for him to concentrate when he studies. He says his mind begins to wander. I hope and pray that if I reach eighty-five years of age, my mind is as good as his.

This has been, for the most part, an uneventful vacation. It began on Monday morning, June 27, and we departed Gainesville in a slight drizzle that had fallen intermittently Sunday night. We were emotionally and physically in need of a vacation. The first night we spent in a third-floor motel room overlooking the Mississippi River in Memphis, Tennessee. From there, it was on to Owensboro to spend a few days with the Ables family. There was a tornado near Owensboro while we were there. Jack and I were on the first hole of the golf course when the big wind came, and we decided not to continue playing. The wind might have helped my game!

On the second hole, it would have been at our backs. However, we quickly returned to Jack's house, and found some of the family in the water heater closet, and the rest in the bathroom. We put everybody into the bathroom, thinking no one should be close to a water heater. It was a rather tense time, but we adults tried to remain calm for the benefit of the kids. I had seen a tornado before. A tornado named Carla had come to Dallas in 1957, and

I remembered the fear and the sound of the wind as I waited to hear that sound again.

We put all four kids in the bathtub and covered them with a mattress. The adults just helplessly stood and waited. All four children seemed to enjoy the "game" of being hidden beneath a mattress, but the four adults prayed silently that our kids would remember this just as a game and nothing more. The tornado struck just across the state line in Evansville, Indiana.

In Madison, West Virginia, we rested at my grandparents' home. They still lived at 212 Walnut Avenue—where I was born. It has always been home to me. It was hot and humid every day (95 degrees and 85 percent humidity). Though it's the time of "dog days," it has been a relaxing time for us.

I asked Dad Pauley about the stone with "Dad's Garden" written on it. His face seemed to glaze over as if he was going back in time.

"You know," he said, "I've written about forty pages about my life, and I still haven't gotten to that part. I want to write it well so that all my children and grandchildren will always remember it." I didn't tell him this, of course, but I just can't wait to read what he is writing.

Sherman and Brazil

October 16, 1977

I was called to Crutchfield Heights Baptist Church in Sherman, Texas. On October 19, I accepted the call to this church. There are some sweet memories from Tabernacle, and some memories that need to be forgotten. Fern Proffer and a few others were a real help to me.

The pulpit committee from Crutchfield Heights included a man who was very laid back. In fact, he excused himself for a few minutes during our interview so he could go "pop his pills." I later learned he had been diagnosed with an incurable type of cancer and had really needed to take his medicine. Bill Rushing made an immediate favorable impression on me.

In fact, the entire committee impressed me. Members of this committee and other people from the church actually came to Tabernacle Church outside Gainesville and helped us move to the parsonage in Sherman. They had a family who took the children to see the *Wizard of Oz* at their house while we were doing the actual moving.

Another family fixed food so there were no meals to be prepared. By the end of the day, everything was in the house and assembled. Pictures were hung on the walls. It was a fantastic one-day complete move. They even had people clean the house we moved from. They said it didn't take long at all because we had kept it clean.

February 14, 1978

Freezing rain, sleet, and snow are supposed to begin here later tonight. If it materializes, this will be the fifth snow we've had this winter. I've come to realize that the weather is something I can do nothing about. So, I don't worry about it.

February 15, 1978

We had three inches of snow—but no major problems.

February 17, 1978

Eight inches of snow fell in almost-blizzard conditions today. This is our fifth major snow, and officially we've had more snow than ever before this winter. This has been the worst winter in Sherman history—and it may not be over yet. However, spring will eventually come.

The snow has almost melted off the roads, but plenty remains in the yards and countryside. I took Matthew to the doctor this morning. He has a low-grade infection that should be cleared up in a few days. This rascal is active even when he doesn't feel well.

March 8, 1978

Snow flurries today, but it is not cold enough for the snow to stick. The flurries, in fact, were beautiful.

July 9, 1979

My hero, my grandfather, died today. Born on October 12, 1891, he had been in bad health for the past two years. He nearly died two years ago. I remember my mother calling me to tell me that and asking us to pray for him not to die. I also remember wondering if that was really what I should have prayed. He suffered for the last two years of his life. Shouldn't our prayers have been for God's will to be done—and not our own? Many thoughts and memories are flooding my mind, and I can't collect them all right now.

What about the stone? Had he finished writing down the story? Had he been so sick that he wasn't able to finish it? Would Mom Pauley be able to tell me?

September 19, 1979

My mind, as well as my pen, is rusty. This past weekend was a little rejuvenating for me. I played in a slow-pitch softball tournament, which our church cohosted with Luella Baptist Church. The pastor and his wife, Jerry and Judy Creek, are good friends of ours. We played at the Luella Bowl, a converted cow pasture that made a pretty fair field. The outfield is still a little treacherous, but the infield is almost smooth. Our team finished second in the tournament. I had seven hits in fourteen at bats and eight runs batted in in our four games. Maybe I'm not a member of the "over-the-hill gang" yet.

My grandfather's funeral, and the resultant family gatherings, didn't present an appropriate time for me to ask Mom Pauley about the "Dad's Garden" stone. Will I ever know what it was he thought it so important for me to know?

February 10, 1981

I am still not able to discipline myself to write each day. I wait for inspiration—and it doesn't come. I've read that writing is 10 percent inspiration and 90 percent perspiration—(or was it that baseball is 10 percent inspiration and 90 percent perspiration?). I'm sure the percentages apply to both.

Yesterday I buried Mrs. Cary and was present a half hour later when a baby was born to one of the young girls related to members of our church. I am involved in a way of life that is sometimes an emotional treadmill.

April 1, 1981

I am on a Braniff 727 bound for Miami from DFW. Forty-one people (including myself and Odell Russell) are bound for Brazil to participate in evangelistic crusades in Curitiba, a city of nearly one million people in southern Brazil. There are twenty-six Baptist churches, and we shall be serving in all of them. Odell and I will be in two of the churches, hoping to be in real revival. I can't comprehend why the Lord wants me, of all people, to be a part of this, but I have the unmistakable conviction that he does. *Excited* is not the word to describe how I feel! Combine the emotions of excitement, elation, apprehension, and wonderment of the ways in which God works, and one might come close to expressing what I feel—but only close!

At eight o'clock, we departed Miami on Varig flight #821 for Rio de Janeiro with stops in Caracas (Venezuela), Manaus, and Brasilia. We've now left the lights of Miami and are out over the ocean, and nothing but darkness is viewable from my window. As I am writing, I can hear snatches of conversation going on all around me, but I am temporarily in my own world of thoughts and written words. I am wondering, as I look out into the darkness, what it will be like to be completely away from my family for two weeks.

April 2, 1981

We made a brief stop in Caracas—landing at 10:58 p.m., and leaving again at 11:45. Some remained on the plane and others got off and roamed around the airport for a few minutes. We landed in Manaus at 3:11. No one got off the plane (we were asked to remain onboard), and we departed again at 4:30 for Brasilia—a two-and-a-half-hour flight.

I've been thinking about the evangelism conference on Friday and Saturday, especially my part in the program. I am seriously thinking of changing the text and message from Acts 4:1–8 to 1 John 5:1–5. I tried (unsuccessfully) to sleep.

We landed in Brasilia at 7:52 and departed at 8:30. From a distance, Brasilia looks like a beautiful, modern city. We arrived in Rio de Janeiro at 10:00 and departed at 12:10 for Curitiba. We changed planes—and the other people on the plane speak only Portuguese. It was rainy and cloudy in Rio, and we were not able to see the Christ of the Mountains statue. My dream since I saw it in a film in sixth grade has been to see it in person. Perhaps we can when we are leaving the country.

We arrived in Curitiba about 1:25, and we had quite a nice reception. People were there to greet us—people from the Baptist churches in which we will be serving. We sang "Minha Patria Para Christo" ("My Country for Christ")—and they appeared to be very appreciative.

At 11:45 p.m., I was waiting for my call to Sondra to go through. I thought I'd record these thoughts concerning tonight's open-air meeting. We went to the "Street of Flowers" to pass out tracts and speak to people. Carlos Gruber began playing his violin, Reginaldo spoke to people who began to gather round (explaining what we were doing), and we sang songs from a little Portuguese songbook. Bill Davis shared his testimony, we sang some more songs, Ricky Hargrave preached, we sang again, I shared my testimony, we sang again, Odell gave his testimony, and one of the local pastors led a prayer.

We tried to deal with those who had questions. We shared copies of our written testimonies, which had been translated into Portuguese. Some decisions were made. I shared with a beautiful young child (age seven or eight). Fernando was a handsome young man who called himself "Harvard" (could it have been Howard?). He had the most searching brown eyes I have ever seen, and a dark-complexioned young man (Thomas) had a most engaging smile. I wish I'd taken pictures of all of them, but I only got Thomas! We went to the seminary for a service that was very inspirational.

April 3, 1981

We went to the governor's palace to see the vice governor of Parana. The governor flew to Japan yesterday. The palace was beautiful inside and out. The vice governor was very friendly. Dr. Truman Wester spoke formally for the group, explaining our purpose for being in Curitiba. Men from the press and television stations were there. Perhaps we shall be on television?

After our meeting with the vice governor, we were shown a room of history. The large room on the first floor had great winding staircases that led to the second floor and formed a sort of balcony overlooking the first floor. A great mural on the north wall told the story of Parana's hardworking people, lumber (Parana Pine is world famous), coffee bean trees, and agriculture (an ox pulling a plow). There were busts of three Brazilian leaders: The middle bust was of Peter I, the first of two Portuguese emperors over Brazil from the Bourbon line. This man's son, Peter II, was emperor when Brazil proclaimed itself a republic. He was brokenhearted at being asked to step aside and returned to Portugal where he died. However, the Brazilians held him in such high regard—he was considered to have been a great leader—they had his bones returned to Brazil. He is still considered a great hero.

From there, we went to the Da Silva Building, which houses the telephone company among other things, and an observation platform (about twenty-four stories high) from which many took pictures of great views of the city. In reality, there are two Curitibas (an industrial city and the residential city). The residential city is breathtaking in beauty.

Lunch at a place in the Italian village consisted of ten courses of meat (including a delicacy "Hump of the Brahma Bull"). The total cost was 365 cruzeiros—about five dollars in American money. Pork, beef, goat, and young chicken were also available.

While the ladies began the evangelism conference, the men had a free afternoon. Odell and I went walking on the Street of Flowers. What a fantastically beautiful and intriguing place. So many people are out walking. There is no vehicular traffic on the very wide avenue.

I could write about tonight's experiences and fill the rest of this book with them. We had a service at the *Templo Cujaru Batista*. Such inspirational singing is a joy to hear—and the friendliness of the people is overwhelming.

It was obvious that many people there had learned a few English words just to help us feel at home. I met Luiz Fernando Marcielo and Manoel Cousa Santos—two very friendly youths. I asked Odell to take a picture of them for me. They are beautiful people. Also I met Jeskiel Freitas and enjoyed trying to talk with him. Paterson had beautiful eyes and smile. Thank you, God, for introducing me to these delightful people.

April 4, 1981

A full day! We began the second day of the evangelism congress at 8:30, and it concluded about ten o'clock that night. Jerry Creek was the opening speaker today. He spoke about rural evangelism. Then, we separated into smaller groups with five small group sessions going on at once. This was also a forty-five-minute session. At eleven o'clock, I spoke on "Evangelizing the Public" ("If We Love God" I John 5:1–5). I used my empty briefcase to provide visual proof of my expertise. An old Brazilian expression is "A man who carries a briefcase is an expert." The empty briefcase provided them with a visual expression. I don't consider myself to be an expert, but the message was well received. Another group meeting lasted until 12:30. Lunch was served in the basement (lower part) of the church. It was an entirely Brazilian meal of various parts of pig with rice and black beans (*feijoada*). There also was cake (meter cake), coffee, mate (tea with lemon), and water. The afternoon and evening sessions consisted of more sermons on evangelism—and more groups.

I've made the acquaintance of so many friendly people today. It is overwhelming to me, and I am nearly in tears even now. How tremendous to be so received! I've made friends with Hamilton Bueno Ribeiro, Junior, Derceu, Estar, Manoel, and "Beto"—Luiz Alberto de Paula Cesar.

Beto is a Catholic who works here in the Hotel Lancaster. I am missing Sondra and the kids fiercely.

April 5, 1981

I sat in on Pastor Arnold's Sunday school class this morning with the intent of just listening to them speak in Portuguese, which they did. Pastor Arnold is originally from England, but he has acquired the ability to speak and understand Portuguese. While I did not understand the conversation at all, I did understand that there was some difference in opinion.

At the end of the lesson, I was asked if I had any comments. I felt led to share with the class a verse of scripture that was on my mind during the lesson: "There is one God, and one mediator between God and man, Jesus Christ" (1 Timothy 2:5). There were astonished looks on the faces of the class members. Pastor Arnold explained they had a discussion about how one gets to heaven, and several class members had suggested that there are several ways. The passage of scripture I felt led to share was exactly what was needed. The *Jardim de Esmeralda Igreja Batista* is already a blessing to me.

July 1, 1981

We are vacationing in Madison, West Virginia (my hometown). I thought it would be different with Dad Pauley no longer here. The last time I was there, one year ago, was to attend his funeral. I was a pallbearer.

But today I am here—and the same spirit pervades the home. Yes, it is different with Dad Pauley not here, but it is still home. The atmosphere and attitude is the same as ever—great. This is still my home. Mom Pauley is still "Mom," and she makes this house a home. No person could ever have a better grandmother than I have, but she is not yet ready to give me the story of the stone. She says that for reasons I'll understand later, she just has a hard time finishing it and letting it go. I am confused.

Meredith's birthday is in three months. She will be six years old, and I have written her a poem. I started on it in the Hotel Lancaster. I wanted to pick up my little girl and hug her closely, but I was in Curitiba while she was in Dallas.

Meredith's Poem

Daughter Meredith

Each night as you kneel at your bed,
We, too, say a prayer as we bow our heads.
After you're hugged and kissed goodnight,
We think of our prayer as we turn out the lights.

We are asking him to fulfill our dreams,
Foolish to others, as they may seem.
But to us, our precious one,
Our life's work completely done.

Though tonight you're a sleepy little girl,
With tousled head and rumpled curl.
In our dreams, we skip the years,
If they come true, we'll shed few tears.

We dream not of wealth or fame,
But, Meredith, never forget his name.
For your wit and beauty, we care a lot,
But love and kindness be not forgot.

We dream of you all dressed in white,
The one you love at your right.
The one day you will turn out a light,
And say this prayer we say tonight.

"For I know the plans I have for you," declares the Lord,
"Plans for welfare and not for calamity,
To give you a future and a hope" (Jeremiah 29:11).
May this be your life verse. Dad.

October 20, 1981

Last week was quite an interesting one here. The rains came—especially on Tuesday and again Thursday night and Friday morning. We had seventeen inches of rain last week (nearly half our yearly norm), and part of the city flooded on Tuesday and Friday. Some people had to evacuate their homes or apartments because of the rising floodwaters that spilled over from the swollen streams. Twice, residents of the Chapel-of-Care Nursing Home had to be rescued and taken to the municipal building or local hospitals.

On Sunday night, our church voted to discontinue church training as it was. It was just as well since our training union had been dead for some time. We never pronounced the eulogy or had the burial service. Somehow, I feel my life is being buried too!

The waters are rising! I am slowly being flooded by waters I cannot escape. My church is dying—and I am dying with it! Lord, is this what my life in ministry is to be—a slow death?

Again I think of Walpole's quotation:

Life is a tragedy to those who feel—a comedy to those who think.

I have been feeling lately, yet I prefer to think *and* feel. I am not complete unless I do both. Actually a person is not complete unless he or she can think, feel, and trust in an invisible means of support—God.

Sondra and I went to Brazil in August 1982 with the group from Sherman. Although we had already moved to Terrell, we had a previous commitment to go with the Sherman group on another mission trip to Curitiba. I was able to introduce Sondra to some of the people I had met on my previous trip. As usual, the hospitality was warm and accepting.

In one of our training sessions before departure, we were told that ladies should never leave their purses on the floor in a public place because this was a signal that the lady was "available." I found myself monitoring Sondra's purse placement frequently.

One of our privileges on the trip to Curitiba was visiting a *favela* (unincorporated area on the fringe of the city). We accepted the hospitality of a host family and drank some hot tea with them. The lady told us her son was in the hospital suffering from hepatitis, but she also emphasized that she had boiled the water for our tea for five minutes. The tea tasted good.

When Sondra told some people about the experience, her language became a little mixed up. Instead of saying we had been to a favela, she was telling people we had been to a bordello for a Bible study. A bordello is a house of ill repute where prostitutes work. While people laughed, and Sondra saw her mistake, I wondered what a Bible study in a bordello would be like.

One night prior to going to the church, Sondra and I were guests for dinner (supper) at the house of one of the church members. After dinner, I went into the bathroom to freshen up. When I finished, I couldn't get out of the bathroom. The door was stuck, and I couldn't get it open. The window had bars on it. Exiting through the window was not a viable option. After about thirty minutes, our hosts were able to open the door. We departed for the church, arriving about twenty-five minutes after the service was supposed to start. People at the church were not overly concerned about our lateness. They were rather amused by my bathroom confinement.

On another occasion, we were visiting with a lady whose small dog wanted my attention. I picked up the little dog and kept it in my lap while I was talking with the lady about our Lord and Savior. I noticed our interpreter was having a rather difficult time not laughing, and I wondered if I was saying something that didn't translate well into Portuguese. After we left, we asked him what was wrong. He thought the little dog I was holding was a rat, and he thought, *This man will do anything—even hold a rat—to tell people about Jesus.* I'm sure I'll be able to use that as a sermon illustration someday.

We arrived back in Terrell the day before Sondra was to report for in-service prior to the beginning of the school year. She had gotten sick in Curitiba, but one of the people who served as interpreters for us was a doctor. She wrote a prescription for Sondra, a combination of medicines that could not be prescribed in the United States, and Sondra got much better.

We spent the night before our departure from Brazil in a hotel in Rio de Janeiro. On the next day, we toured *Corcovado* (the statue of Christ) on *Pan de Azul* (Sugarloaf Mountain). Riding up to the top of the mountain on a tram was not too difficult, but getting Sondra off that tram was a bit of a difficulty. Between the docking platform and the edge of the tram was a space of about four inches that one had to step across to exit the tram. Sondra was not going to make that step, fearing she would fall through that space into the bay below. Rather, she was just going to ride back down to the ground and wait for us to return. I convinced her that I wouldn't allow her to fall, and she hung on for dear life.

She was not comfortable the entire time we were on that mountain. After we stepped off the tram, people took our picture with Sugarloaf as a background. The statue of Christ with his arms outstretched overlooking Rio is impressive beyond description. The symbolism of his protection over Rio is as impressive to me now as it was when I was in sixth grade. The guide explained that the architect built a stairway inside the statue and carved his name on the inside where the heart of Jesus would be located. "How much more important it will be," I shall explain in a sermon, "that Jesus's name be imprinted upon our hearts."

As we were leaving the mountain, we were presented with the opportunity to purchase the picture imprinted upon a saucer. We bought it, of course. The pictures Sondra took upon the mountain will probably all be blurry because she was shaking so much when she took them. When I got close to the retaining wall, she would encourage me not to go any closer. She was really scared.

In the afternoon, we went to Copacabana Beach before going to the airport. Though she was wearing hose, Sondra couldn't resist the temptation to step into the water. She carried Brazilian sand in her shoes all the way back to Terrell. So did I—but not as much.

Sermons

Dry Brooks and Empty Flour Barrels
Emmanuel Baptist Church of Terrell, Texas

April 25, 1982

Alexander Whyte, the great Scottish preacher and biographer of many Bible characters, introduces Elijah to us with these words: "The prophet Elijah towers up like a mountain in Gilead above all other prophets. There is a solitary grandeur about Elijah that is all his own. There is a mystery and an unearthliness about Elijah that is all his own. There is a volcanic suddenness and a volcanic violence, indeed, about Elijah—descents upon us and his disappearances from us. He was a Mount Sinai of a man with a heart like a thunderstorm" (1 Kings 17:1–24).

Indeed he was! Elijah was a man of God. He was a man of faith. He was a man of prayer and great courage. He did ascend and descend upon the scene—coming and then disappearing with a volcanic suddenness. He appeared in the court of Ahab, the king of Israel, one day (having lived in the deserts and mountains of Gilead prior to that) and threw down the gauntlet before the king. He said, "Sir, I have come to declare unto you that there is not going to be another drop of rain upon this earth until *I* give the word," and, with that said, he disappeared.

Politically, socially, and religiously, Israel was in a state of uproar at the time. Under the neglectful leadership of King Ahab, the situation had deteriorated in an unbelievable way. "And Ahab the son of Omri did evil in the sight of the Lord more than all who were before him" (1 Kings 16:30). That tells us what we need to know about Ahab. You'll remember he had a little help in his evil, in that he was married to the conniving, lying, slanderous, unscrupulous Jezebel, and she was a follower of the religion of Baal, the Canaanite god. She was a follower of Baal, and she believed strongly that everybody else in the land ought to be a worshiper of Baal as well. She set about to wipe from the face of the earth the worship of Jehovah God and to make the worship of Baal the religion of the entire land.

As we read through this story, we are prone to say, "Well, is God going to let this go unnoticed? Is God going to let this wicked king and queen go unchecked and not call their hand?" Of course not! Out there in the wilds of Gilead, God was getting his man ready. There in that wilderness wasteland, God was hammering out his will in the heart and soul of his "Mount Sinai of a man," and Elijah appeared on the scene one day, as already indicated, and announced the coming drought.

Now you must understand! You must understand that the challenge of Elijah was more than a mere challenge to Ahab, the king. In essence, it was a challenge to Jezebel and her god of Baal, and all that he stood for. For, you see, the god of Baal was supposed to be the god of fertility. It was he who supposedly brought the rains from heaven. He supposedly caused the dew to come. It was he who caused the mist to cover the earth and caused the land to produce.

Elijah was saying, "King Ahab, I want you to realize that Jezebel's god, Baal, is not in control here. Rather, Jehovah God is in control, and I'm going to prove that to you by telling you that there is not going to be any more rain these years, except by my word. And if Baal is in control, you'll have rain. But he isn't, and you won't until I say the word."

Then Elijah disappeared. He disappeared because God told him to go underground. In verse three, he says, "Get thee hence, and turn thee eastward, and hide thyself by the brook Cherith, that is before Jordan" (1 Kings 17:3). Now you must understand—please don't miss this—that the underground experience, the hideaway at this point, was God's idea and not Elijah's. In fact, if Elijah had his way about it, he probably would have preferred to remain right out in the forefront, looking Jezebel right in the eye and saying, "My dear queen, let us settle this matter once and for all." He did that a little later.

But God seemed to be saying, "Elijah, there are times for challenges! There are times for confrontations! But there are times when you need to be alone with *me.* I want you to go to the Brook Cherith, and there I want you to hide. I want you to drink the water from the brook, and I will command the ravens to feed you there." In obedience to the command of God, Elijah went to the Brook Cherith.

Some of us have mental pictures that we've created of some of these scenes that are described for us in the Bible. I have imagined here a beautiful little hideaway by a babbling mountain stream near which are multicolored, fragrant wildflowers and rich green foliage—and I have seen with my mind's eye Elijah communing with the Lord. That's not the way it was! That area where God sent Elijah had no babbling mountain brooks. The Brook Cherith was not a babbling spring of water; it was a trickle of water cutting through the floor of the desert. In fact, *Cherith* means "cutting place." The water that came up there was polluted to begin with.

God said, "Elijah, I'm going to send you to that Godforsaken place out in the middle of the desert where there is nothing but a trickle of water that comes up through the desert floor. I want you to drink that water, and I will command the ravens to bring you food."

Once again, we've created mental images, haven't we? The raven is a beautiful, coal-black bird. I think we see the ravens showing up every morning and every evening punctually with a hunk of sirloin and a piece of freshly baked bread in their beaks. Let me tell you again that is not the way it happened.

Do you know what ravens eat? They eat the remains— the putrefying flesh—left behind by hyenas and the jackals in the desert. They ate the food that was discarded over the city walls—the garbage. Out there with the polluted water and leftover food, God was humbling Elijah. Elijah was on the cutting edge in the refiner's fire at Zarephath and at Cherith. There could never have been a Carmel had there not been a Cherith. There could never have been a crown had there not been a cross first of all.

Cherith was a place of Elijah's divine appointment with God! It was no accident that he ended up at Cherith. God, in a sense, was saying, "Elijah, out there in that desert, you and I are going to do business that we can't do anywhere else."

Now let me say this to you because it is the truth of God. Every one of us has our "Cherith experiences." There are times when God puts us out there on a limb and then saws it off behind us. We feel as if we have been forsaken by God. There are times when we feel humbled and feel the agony and experience of being alone in the journey along the road of life.

I beg you to hear me when I say we are not here by accident. We may be here by God's appointment. He might hammer out in our souls that which he wants us to do and bring to pass out of our experience.

God was getting Elijah ready, but he didn't leave him there. After Elijah had been there a while, the brook ran dry. "And the word of the Lord came unto him, saying, 'Arise, get thee to Zarephath, which belonged to Zidon, and dwell there: behold, I have commanded a widow woman there to sustain thee!'"

That is a wonderful change of scenery, isn't it? Do you know where Zarephath is? It's over on the Mediterranean coast. You say, "Aha, from that Godforsaken place in the middle of the desert, God is going to take him to a villa down on the Mediterranean." Not exactly.

Zarephath was a part of the country of Zidon, which won't mean anything to you until you realize that the king of Zidon was Jezebel's father. Zidon was her native country.

God is saying, "Elijah, I want you to cross this scorching desert and march yourself right down to the very doorstep of Jezebel and open up shop."

And in obedience to the command of God, Elijah crossed that desert and arrived finally in Zarephath. When he arrived at the gates of the city, God showed him the widow God had promised would sustain Elijah. She was gathering sticks. He broke all the rules of the day by asking her for a drink of water. That was not done in those days! Men and women did not communicate in public, especially not when they were strangers. He asked the woman for a drink of water, which was an act of humiliation.

The woman said, "I'll get you a drink of water." She turned to get the drink of water.

As she did so, Elijah said, "By the way, would you also bring me a morsel of bread to eat with that drink of water?"

When he asked that question, she stopped dead in her tracks. "A morsel of bread?" she said. "I am but a widow woman. I have been to my meal bowl, and there is not a handful of meal left in the bowl. I'm out here gathering these sticks so I can go back to the house, make a fire, take that handful of meal and the little bit of oil I have left in my cruse, and I'm going to cook the last drop of provisions I have left on the earth for my boy and me. Then my boy and I will sit down, like some other people are doing, and starve to death."

You see, famine gripped the land. There was no water—no rain—for well-nigh three years now. Elijah was saying, "I want you to take the last meal and oil that you have in your possession and cook it for me." The woman was saying, "Man of God, do you know what you are asking? Before my son and I die, aren't we at least entitled to this one little bit of luxury—this one last piece of bread? Would you take this from us?"

Elijah said, "Listen, my dear lady. God has given me a promise. He promised that if you'll cook that bread for me, your meal bowl will never go empty as long as there is famine in the land."

He convinced her. She fixed that bread for him and, according to the scriptures, her meal bowl never went empty again. Never!

Cherith was a cutting place for Elijah. God was hammering away—chiseling at the soul and heart of this man. God sent him over to Zarephath. You'll be interested to know that Zarephath means "a place of refining." Just as a sculptor chisels away at the stone and gets a shape from it, sands it down, polishes it, and refines it, God was continuing to test and refine the soul of his prophet, Elijah, at Zarephath.

The lesson is this—and I beg you to hear it—as long as that widow held on to that handful of meal, that was exactly what she had—a handful of meal. When given to God, it was multiplied again and again and again.

There is a sequel in the New Testament about a boy with five barley loaves and two fishes. As long as he kept it, it was only lunch enough for one boy. But when it was given to Jesus, it was multiplied five thousand times over—enough to feed a multitude.

Can't we see it? The only thing that really matters in life is what we are willing to give to the Lord. What we give to him he gives back many times over. That which we lose is that which we grasp to ourselves and demand for ourselves.

What God began at the Brook Cherith, he continued at Zarephath, preparing Elijah for the Mount Carmel experience. When your Cherith experiences come, how do you respond to them? When God gets you out there in that lonely place where you feel your faith has been tested to the very limit, when you feel that you can't go on, do you realize that what you may call an accident may be an appointment with God?

Out there at your brook, God may want to do something in your soul! He may cause you to leave your Cherith and humble yourself at Zarephath, being refined for some great purpose. When your brook runs dry and your flour barrel is nearly empty, God may be testing you—and preparing you—for greater things! Ask him about it, won't you? He'll answer you.

The Fence-Straddling Governor

(Emmanuel Baptist Church)

May 2, 1982

1 Kings 18:1–19

They looked to be a menacing group of people! As they surrounded the new boy on the playground, they began explaining that every new boy in the seventh grade was required to "ride the fence." This was done by straddling the fence while male classmates shook the fence. As this tradition was being explained, the boy was surveying the chain-link fence, the condition of which was not at all to his liking. Its foundation was rather loose, and several strands of fence were no longer attached to the top pole. While he studied the fence, the explanation continued. He who was able to stay on the fence and endure the effects of the ride was accepted into the inner circle of the class. He who was not able to stay on and suffer the effects of the ride was to be branded as an outcast.

The new boy did not have a choice about whether or not to ride. His choice involved only whether the ride would be voluntary or by force. The new boy kept trying to politely decline the honor that was to be bestowed upon him without much success. "It's a tradition," they said. "Everybody rides the fence. There are no exceptions."

To this statement, the boy replied, "Today either part of my body will be broken *or* your tradition will be broken. Since the tradition means nothing to me, it is what will be broken."

Later, after he successfully resisted the attempts of several boys to get him mounted on the fence, they asked, "Why did you refuse? Every new guy straddles the fence. Every new guy is initiated by riding the fence. No one has ever refused. Why did you refuse?"

"First of all, it's dangerous. Secondly, why should I allow that just because other people have been silly enough to do it?"

For the boy—who happened to be me—straddling the fence was dangerous. Another kind of fence straddling is also very dangerous. We learn that today from the story of Elijah when he encountered Obadiah, governor of the house of King Ahab.

First, let me briefly recount Elijah's story to you. As Ahab became king of Israel and married Jezebel, wicked daughter of Ethbaal, king of Tyre and Sidon (Zidon), God was preparing a man in the wilds of Gilead whom he was going to use to stop the wickedness of Ahab and Jezebel. God sent Elijah to the court of King Ahab with a message:

There will be not a drop of rain these days until my God so allows.

This was a challenge to Ahab, Jezebel, and Baal (supposedly the god of fertility who controlled rainfall). God sent Elijah to hide by the Brook Cherith, providing for him for six months, by influencing the ravens to bring him bread and flesh to eat. When the Brook Cherith dried up, God was ready to send Elijah to Zarephath for three years, so that he could finish honing him and refining him for the conflicts ahead. A widow who God blessed because of her faith sustained him there.

So, we know Elijah. We know Ahab. We're familiar with Jezebel. The Bible now introduces us to another man in this continuing drama. Obadiah is his name.

There had been no rain upon that part of the earth for three and a half years. We know what it's like to go without rain for several weeks. Can you imagine what it must have been like to go three and a half solid years (at least forty-two months) without one drop of rain, one drop of dew, or any form of water to refresh or replenish the earth?

Streams became dried-up trenches. There was no green grass available. Shrubs and trees were withered and dying. There was a severe situation in the land. The inspired writer said, "There was a sore famine in Samaria" (1 Kings 18:26). The situation was critical and crucial.

As is usually the case, the royal palace was the last place to be affected by this. If there was any grain in the land, you can imagine where it was to be stored. If there was any water available, you can imagine where it was. When the pinch began to be felt in the royal palace Ahab said, "Obadiah, we do not want our horses and our mules to die."

Interestingly enough, it seemed to be all right for all these *people* to die—but not Ahab's horses and mules. Ahab said, "We'll go search for green grass and water, Obadiah. You take one half of the country, and I'll take the other half."

Obadiah was the governor of the king's house. He was like the secretary of state or the prime minister. King Ahab was the weak-kneed, spineless king. Jezebel was the ruthless, conniving, unscrupulous queen. Elijah was the desert-bred firebrand of a prophet from the living God. Now, we see Obadiah, the governor, in charge of the king's affairs. What do we know about this man?

We know that he apparently was a rather gifted man, a man with skills and talents. I base this belief on the fact that he had been made governor of the land. Kings and queens became kings or queens by inheritance or by marriage alliances. Governors were elevated to their positions because they were men of skills and talents. He was on the ball.

The Bible also tells us that he was a man who feared the Lord greatly. This is illustrated by the fact that he hid and provided for one hundred prophets of God when Jezebel was oppressing and having many prophets killed. This raises—and brings into focus—a baffling question: *How could Obadiah have been trusted by a wicked king and at the same time have it said that he feared the Lord."*

I'll give you my evaluation. Here is a man who is trying to play on both sides of the street. He's trying to play both ends against the middle. He wanted to remain governor of all Israel while having some fear of the Lord in his heart. He wanted to do what he felt God wanted him to do, but he didn't want to do it badly enough to come out and say categorically, "I am on the Lord's side."

We have a term for a person like that. When someone does not take a solid position on either side, we call him a "fence straddler." Obadiah wanted to be the king's governor and a faithful servant of God at the same time. Now that's an uncomfortable position to occupy, but Obadiah chose that position for himself. That's him—Obadiah, the fence straddler.

Under Ahab's directions, Obadiah set out to tour half the country, looking for green grass and water for the king's horses and mules, while Ahab scoured the other half of the country.

In the middle of the road, Obadiah met the last man on the face of this earth he wanted to see. Elijah appeared again with almost volcanic suddenness, without announcement or notice, right there in the middle of the road. Obadiah knew it was the man who had proclaimed judgment on Israel by saying there would be no water for three years until he gave the word.

Obadiah was sure that Elijah was dead. He hadn't been seen or heard from in three and a half years! Can you imagine, and this fact is alluded to in these verses, the determination that Jezebel must have had in trying to hunt down Elijah and have him killed. The palace guards, secret police, CIA, FBI, everybody was on the lookout for Elijah, but they couldn't find him. Do you know why?

They couldn't find him because he was right near home. God had sent Elijah to Zarephath—the old stomping ground of Jezebel. He was right there under their noses, and they couldn't find him.

Elijah said, "Obadiah, I want you to go tell Ahab that I want to see him."

Obadiah was not too enthused about the idea.

Elijah said, "Go tell the king I want a second audience with him."

Obadiah had problems with this. He said, "When I go tell Ahab that Elijah wants to see him, and I bring him here, the Spirit of the Lord may well have taken you someplace else. You'll be gone, and he'll kill me. Don't you know he had soldiers searching all over for you because of the trouble that has come upon the land? He has even consulted heads of other nations and had them swear an oath that you weren't in those nations! If I bring him here, and you're not here, he'll kill me!"

Obadiah had a second problem with this proposition: Ahab might say, "How come you know where he is? You knew where he was all the time, didn't you?" Obadiah was between a rock and a hard place.

Elijah said, "I give you my word, Obadiah. I will be here when you return."

I point this out because it is a significant, pivotal point in the story. For the first time in his life, Obadiah faced a man he could trust. For his entire professional life, he had lived among cynics. He had spent time with people in the king's court who could pat him on the back with one hand and pick his pocket with the other.

Obadiah could see through the idolatrous paganism that had infiltrated the land. And now a rather unconventional man said, "Obadiah, you can trust me. When I say I'll be here when you get back, you can count on it."

Something was triggered within Obadiah's heart. *I can trust him*, he thought. A moment of truth presented itself, and Obadiah chose to do what Elijah asked. He persuaded Ahab to meet Elijah where Elijah wanted to meet.

He must have been persuasive! The usual practice for someone desiring to have an audience with the king would have been for them to come to him. He was, after all, the king! But such was not the case here.

Ahab (the king) went to where Elijah was awaiting him. And Elijah threw down the gauntlet again. "If Baal is God, let's worship him. If Jehovah is God, let's worship him." In other words, we're going to have to get off this fence.

We don't hear very much from Obadiah after this, but there are three lessons evident in what we know of Obadiah's life:

> Fence straddlers never amount to very much as far as kingdom service is concerned. This is the only mention of this Obadiah in the entire Bible. Though he was Ahab's governor, he apparently never accomplished much for God.
>
> There is a New Testament example of this in Revelation 3:14–16. Jesus, in his letter to the church at Laodicea is saying, "I know your ways. You are neither hot nor

cold. I wish you were either one or the other. But, you are lukewarm and you make me sick" (Perry's paraphrase). The Laodiceans were trying to be friends of the Lord and of the world at the same time. That just doesn't work. You can't hobnob with the devil's crowd on Saturday night and with the Lord's crowd on Sunday morning and be comfortable in both places. One who tries to do that is straddling the fence. He needs to get off the fence on one side or the other.

Such things as faith and courage are contagious. They can be "caught and taught." Why did Obadiah deliver this rather dangerous message to Ahab? How was he able to persuade Ahab to meet Elijah? I believe the courage of Elijah was contagious and Obadiah caught some of it.

The simplest act of obedience can be monumental as far as kingdom service is concerned. Obadiah did persuade Ahab to meet Elijah. Elijah issued the challenge— and the resultant confrontation on Mount Carmel resulted in great revival.

I'm going to coin a phrase here. If this isn't already a word, then I'm going to invent a word. Are we ever "Obadious" in our outlook? Do we ever straddle the fence—not come off the fence on one side or the other? Do we ever try to be a friend to the world and a friend to the friends of God at the same time? Are we trying to straddle the fence in our relationship to Christ?

God says, "Friend, come off that fence on one side or the other—but come off." Fear the Lord! Serve him with all your heart! Be all he wants you to be!

I remember Joshua's charge, don't you? "Choose ye this day whom you are going to serve! As for me and my house, we will serve the Lord."

Jesus said, "If you're not for me, you're against me!"

Who today is on the Lord's side? If you're not, wouldn't you like to be?

Our Blessings from God

Children are a blessing from God. Every time I hear of or see a newborn baby I am reminded that God is still delivering miracles. We have two who are real blessings to us. Sometimes I think of them as "Thunder" and "Sunrise."

Matthew is "Thunder." He is not exactly bombastic, but he is enthusiastically lively.

As we were driving back to Sherman after visiting Terrell in view of a call to Emmanuel Baptist Church, he said "Dad, we're not really moving here, are we? This town has too many liquor stores." He remembered I was one of the ministers in Sherman who had been involved in the movement to prevent private clubs from operating. Grayson County was a dry county, and we felt restaurants that were selling private club memberships and serving alcoholic beverages to those members were skirting the law. Kaufman County, in which Terrell is located, is a wet county. Liquor stores can operate legally. "This town has too many liquor stores," he said. He was right.

This is the same boy I recorded in the parsonage at Tabernacle Baptist near Gainesville. I had been trying to record some music by Ethel Waters, which I intended to play in my office at the church as I was studying. I kept hearing Matthew, and I knew his voice was getting onto that tape. I said, "Boy, I'm going to get your bottom."

"No," he screamed, "I'm gonna get your bottom." The commotion was recorded, including his wildly enjoyable laugh when I caught him.

This is the same boy who enthusiastically encouraged our Border collie, Callie (short for "Calpurnia") to attack the neighbor's guineas when they came into our yard. I was sure that Callie wouldn't bother those birds. I had taught her better. Matthew was a better encourager than I was a discourager. Sometimes we would have to tie Callie to a tree when the guineas were loose. I accepted the neighbor's displeasure when his guineas would be killed and would reimburse him for their cost. However, when he called to complain that his three hundred-pound pig had been killed, I had to express my doubts about Callie being able to do that. She was just six months old.

This boy gave his sister her first haircut. Naturally a second haircut had to be administered—by a professional. Meredith really wasn't pleased with that haircut either.

Matthew loved his Morgan grandparents very much. He really didn't get a chance to have equal exposure to my mother; her last husband didn't like kids. They should be seen and not heard. Believe me, Matthew was seen and heard. When we had a meal with his Morgan grandparents, if he didn't like something on his plate, he would sneak the plate off the table and put it under the bed. Sometimes that plate wasn't found for several days.

Once when he was a teenager, Matthew had to take our cat to the vet. We didn't have a carrier. Matthew put the cat inside a pillowcase. The vet needed twenty minutes to get the cat settled enough to treat her. We had named the cat Sharekhan, after a tiger in Rudyard Kipling's *Jungle Book*. It had been several years since I last read the book, and I had apparently forgotten that the tiger was very vicious. Matthew helped her earn her name by doing various things such as placing her on top of the house. Matthew is not an introverted boy.

Even though my first impression of Meredith was "she sure has a good set of lungs," I don't think I have ever heard her get loud since her birth. She did learn to cope with Thunder and his antics in a way that allowed him to keep his dignity while deciding to stop bothering that girl.

Meredith is like the sunrise. She doesn't call attention to herself, but she is a trendsetter just by being herself. She is sometimes a Daddy's girl. After we had been at Emmanuel a few months, it was time for Vacation Bible School. At the carnival on the last day of Bible School, I sat in the dunking booth. When she saw what people were doing to her daddy, getting him all wet, she became visibly upset. She wanted to be my protector.

When we lived in Sherman Meredith attended the Crutchfield Heights School right across Dewey Street from the church. She got out of school at two o'clock and would come over to the church office.

Once I was a few minutes late coming out of the church to walk her across the street. I had let time sneak up on me. Hearing unusual noises from kids, I immediately went out of the building to see what was happening. Kids told me there was a possum out there wandering around. I didn't like the situation. Possums are nocturnal. I got the kids inside the church building and called the animal control section of the Sherman Police Department. I kept the kids inside the church until animal control captured the possum and took him away.

Meredith was concerned that the possum might be hurt. I explained that the doctors would have to examine the animal to see if it was sick or if a car had hit it. She wanted to go see if the possum was okay. How could I explain that the possum would have to be euthanized in order for them to test for rabies? We did go to the animal control center, but we didn't get to see the possum. We did, however, see a little puppy that needed a home. I could see in Meredith's eyes that she wanted to give that puppy a home. Probably I did too. A piece of advice if you are reading this and thinking about adopting a puppy—check the size of his feet!

I won't say that Wags was large. However, when we moved to Terrell, Wags pulled the Volkswagen. Okay, maybe that is a bit of an exaggeration, but she could have done so if we had the need.

One of our deacons found a house for us to rent when we first moved to Terrell on the Saturday before the first Sunday in February 1982. As we were moving in, two kids from across the street came over and introduced themselves. They were helpful with carrying things. As they helped, we learned that they were also curious. The previous occupants of the house had also been a minister and his family. They wanted to see if we were anything like that family. The preacher had killed his wife, his kids, set fire to the house, and then killed himself. When the mother of those kids realized they were at our house, she immediately came over and was very apologetic. Meredith was first to assure them that I wouldn't do anything to hurt the family. I was very amused with those kids, and I was touched by Meredith's sincerity and concern.

Six months later, we found a house to buy. Some extensive work was needed in the part of the house that was to be Meredith's room. We tore out old carpet, thoroughly cleaned the room, and applied some Raggedy Ann wallpaper to the walls. That became the most pleasant room in the house. We got a daybed for Meredith. It seemed as if the sun always rose in that room first. That is the affect Meredith has on people.

November 9, 1984

Spending the night with Sondra's parents, I am thinking and wondering why I am not heartbroken? We buried Ross Perry, my father, today at eleven at Restland in the Acadia Park section. My sisters had tears. My brothers had tears. I was the comforter and not the comforted. Several people from my church—Emmanuel Baptist in Terrell—came to the funeral, which was an uplifting thing for me. They are so thoughtful!

I realize that I needed not much comfort today because I have experienced his death as a father to me long ago. I probably should say I was dead to him—rejected long ago. My tears came then. I can't help thinking about what might have been.

An idea for a "life vignette" came to me during the graveside service. I was reminded of a piece I wrote during my college days and was never satisfied with. I am trying it again with a few changes.

A Gathering of Flies

Though the season was officially over, summer was not even faltering. There were still sun-parched days and sultry nights, freeing the frenzied hordes of flies and straining to hear a muted splashing in the shallow, stagnant pond near the nursing home. Though the days were supposed to be shorter, they seemed to be longer now, and the passing from dawn to dusk was slower still. The days entwined beneath the shadows until they became an endless, rooted maze of time. The night approached with cricket sounds, and an unfamiliar breeze brushed the moss against the mire of the pond. In a not-so-remote grove near the stagnant pond, a room, tottering on its rusted timbers, jutted out behind the rest of the nursing home.

A gathering of flies surrounded the room and shattered its silence with a constant buzzing cadence. Within, a faded calendar fluttered its pages in the cooling breath of air and shed a cruel, laughing shadow on the opposite wall. There, pushed against the corner, was a ragged bed and the languishing figure of a dying man. He was a miner, born in the green valley that was now a brackish gray, and cradled within the braided boughs of thick mountainside trees. He was a weary, suffering man whose entire life was centered in pick mining in the bosom of Mother Earth (a bosom to which he feared he would soon be returning permanently) and the rhythmic rocking of the coal train, and whose name was recorded only on the miner's slate and in the bartender's brain.

He knew that death was waiting at the back screen, fumbling with the latch. The miner groaned and clutched his stomach in a wave of nausea. He doubled up his body in a knotted form until his knees cast shadows on the floor below.

Why don't they help me? Don' they know I'm dying?

He cast a furtive glance at the screen and was relieved to find the latch still in place. He kept his eyes trained on the latch in a way that seemed to suggest that it wouldn't dare move while he was looking.

The hands of a watched clock never move, and a watched pot never boils.

A second wave of pain shot through his back and pushed him so hard that he was hanging precariously off the bed. He sprawled across his own shadow, one foot still caught upon the bed, an arm pinned beneath his twisted chest. The calendar laughed again, and the cracked ceiling looked down upon death's prey.

Death still fumbled at the latch. The miner's eyes, dazed with pain, were still riveted upon the latch. For a brief moment, he thought he saw the latch tremble.

Is it moving or am I imagining? Why can't I breathe?

No one came to stand the deathwatch. No one came with gentle tears to curse the miner's impending death. Still, in that not-so-remote grove, a final tribute would be paid. The weeping trees would bend their heads, and the crickets would raise their chords in sad farewell. The grove would feel the loss of its simple child before anyone else would know.

The breeze stopped. The calendar hung crucified on its rusty nail, its laughing ceased. In the middle of the floor, the miner made one last attempt to move his arm. The pain became agony as he grabbed the bed, and from within, he could see—but not feel—his body back on the mattress.

As he struggled, the latch broke. A dark shadow slipped stealthily into the room. Accompanied by the jungle-like rhythm of throaty frogs, the shadow made its way to the crumpled figure on the bed. The pain ceased as the icy fingers of death passed over the form.

From within the room came an outward rush of air. There was no sound. As darkness descended, only the gathering of flies against the screen shattered the perfect calm of death.

Changes

November 26, 1984

"Things will look better in the morning." I've heard that hundreds of times before, and I probably have said it a few times. I tried telling myself that last night, but I found it hard to believe. When a man doesn't believe himself, he might have a credibility problem.

Before she went to sleep, I tried to tell Sondra what I was feeling. However, I realized that she was only hearing my words and not the feelings behind them. I can't expect her to understand or comprehend feelings or emotions that I can't understand or explain.

I feel a combination of worthlessness, despair, discouragement, frustration, and anger—like I am either going to give up and die mentally (or spiritually) or explode in a big sudden burst. I can't seem to find an outlet for the emotions that are building inside me. I can't find a logical reason to explain this emotional chaos.

As I was preaching last night, I had the eerie feeling that no one was listening. It was as though I was trying to reach into a world to which I was not allowed—the world where the rest of the congregation was residing. I couldn't even follow the outline I had prepared for myself. In frustration, I just stopped and gave the invitation. Two people came forward to move their membership letters to our church.

I need a way to express aggression—a constructive way—so that it won't be expressed destructively.

December 3, 1984

Sondra has advised me to put some of my writings in book form and give them as Christmas gifts. That might be a viable thing to do if I can find enough to complete a booklet—and if I can find time to type them. She also suggested I submit "A Gathering of Flies" to a Christian magazine for publication. Maybe I will. I deliberately made it short, tight, and concise. Of course, if anyone wants to publish it, they will probably want it expanded. I guess I can submit and see. I am trying to learn to write better—to make writing more than a hobby.

Butterflies in the Wind

(To Sondra)

A child is a butterfly in the wind:
Some can fly higher than others:
But each one flies the best that it can.
Why compare one against the other?
Each one is different.
Each one is special.
Each one is beautiful.
Of such is the kingdom of God.

June 4, 1985

Kimberly Jane Phillips was buried yesterday. I baptized her four years ago when there was a death to the control of Satan over her burial with Christ and resurrection to newness of life in him. Because of that, her physical death Friday (drowning) and her burial yesterday are not events to cause everlasting grief—but there is grief nevertheless. A fourteen-year-old girl made one wrong step, stepped into a hole in Lake Texoma, and paid her life for it. Brother

Eddie said, "She had an appointment." Eddie! When is my appointment? Is it near?

August 8, 1985

I wrote this down on the back of a note sent home from school by the nurse suggesting Matthew have a vision examination. I guess this was the only thing handy when I thought of these things:

A friend is one who knows you as you are, understands what you've been, accepts who you've become, and still gently invites you to grow.

August 11, 1985

The Fernwood reunion is always the second Saturday of August (since 1970). I nearly always dread going, but I am glad I went after I get there. Yesterday Bro, John McGukin, and his family were there. It was good so see them after twenty-three years,

Today I know I may be preaching one of my final sermons as pastor at Emmanuel. Full of conflicting emotions, I am not yet prepared to resign, but know it is almost inevitable. I am in a vacuum.

August 29, 1985

It's been a busy two weeks. I did tender my resignation to be effective after Sunday, September 1. There are many adjustments to be made. It is difficult to cope with the few people at church who "love me so much" now that I have resigned. I've wondered at the way that "love" was expressed before. Love like that could kill a person.

I will miss the others (the quiet majority). Being a teacher instead of a preacher will take some getting used to for me as well as for others (Sondra and the kids especially). But it is what I feel led to do, and I can't let my concern about what others think keep me from doing what I have to do.

May 10, 1986

I am at Ennis High School to judge a UIL (University Interscholastic League) modern oratory contest. This school year has been quite a learning experience for me. There are many areas of stress and frustration. Veteran teachers have said this has been the most frustrating and stressful year of their careers. TECAT is the main culprit. The stress of preaching ministry has prepared me well for this.

There have also been many pleasant moments this year. I look forward to improving as a teacher. I'm happy in what I am doing, but there have been financial difficulties.

June 30, 1986

I've just learned that Mom Pauley died today. My grandmother is dead not quite six years after Dad Pauley died. I miss them!

July 2, 1986

I am on Delta Flight 377 bound for Huntington via Cincinnati, Ohio. Mom's funeral is tomorrow, and I am quite unexpectedly going to be there. Our financial situation made it impossible to go, and I really was disappointed. However, when I arrived home last night from umpiring a baseball game, Sondra said Raymond Lawrence had called and told her some friends from Emmanuel wanted me to go and would pay the way for me to fly up for the funeral. That's why I am 39,000 feet up in the air instead of in linguistics class at ETMCF in Garland.

I always seem to be receiving help from Raymond, and I can't recall ever being able to help him or do something for him.

My mind has settled some now. The first few minutes of flight saw my mind filled with pictures of a plane developing trouble and plummeting to earth. The uneasiness may stem from the fact that I have no control over this plane. In fact, there are very few things over which I do have control.

I changed planes in Cincinnati, and my mind has been to the movies again. I wouldn't want to say this plane is small, but when the minibus arrived at the sight of embarkation, they were still unfolding the plane I was to get on.

They were gassing it up from a five-gallon can. It really eased my mind when the pilot/flight attendant/steward (all the same person) remarked, "It usually takes all five gallons and fumes to get us there."

I'm sitting in the tail section behind the other two passengers, and I can read the instrument panel in the cockpit. Right next to the little radar screen is a little phone that reads: *Dial a Prayer.* I'm freaked out because the pilot and copilot are holding hands!

The other two passengers don't seem to be at all perturbed by this situation. I have noticed though that they seem to be flying a little higher than the plane—probably with the help of whatever is in that little flask they keep passing back and forth.

We are descending right into the side of a hill; fortunately, there is a little landing strip. We may kill several hundred ants when we touch down. I hope we survive!

After the plane stopped, I am relieved to see that the pilot and copilot are man and wife. They are gently coaxing the other two passengers off the plane.

July 4, 1986

The funeral yesterday was beautiful. Reverend White of Mount Vernon Baptist Church in Hurricane was very sensitive.

The ride over to Madison was pleasant. I rode with Suzanna, Joe, Gene, and Timmy (Gene's son).

What happened to the stone? Did they ever write down what they wanted me to know? If so, where is it? If not, how will I ever know why that stone was so important? What is the significance of "Dad's Garden" inscribed on the stone?

Everyone in the van is looking at me, and I realize they are awaiting an answer to a question I haven't even heard! I had to apologize and explain that I was lost in some memories. They understood because we all have our various memories.

July 5, 1986

"I will lift up mine eyes unto the hills, from whence cometh my help" (Psalms 121:1).

All true help comes from the Lord.
It is appointed unto man once to die and then the judgment" (Hebrews 9:27).
Lord, help us to remember when we first met,
And see the strong love that grew between us,
To see the good within the other,
And find the answers
To all our problems.
Help us to say the kind and loving things and make us
Big enough to ask forgiveness of one another.
Help us keep our marriage and children in your hands.

My Father's Hand

Dedicated in memory of Lola Faye Pauley, my grandmother, who not only is in my Father's Hand but now is in my Father's House. Published in *American Poetry Anthology, 1986, volume VI, Number 5.*

During the insecure moments of my life
When I feel unprotected and defenseless,
I fear I will loosen my grip on my Heavenly Father's
hand …
As a flash of panic sets in
And my soul grows disquieted within,
I hear the Father's voice
Speak his soothing words of comfort,
"Don't be anxious about how firm the grip
Of your hand is on mine …
For my Hand is holding yours,
And nothing will cause it to slacken.
Even in your most troubled hour
I will not allow you to pull away."

September 1985

Robert Hastings, former editor of a Baptist paper in Illinois, wrote an article several years ago in one of the Southern Baptist publications. In this article, he wrote that most people have a dream in which they enter into a passenger train and embark upon a long journey. On this journey, they look out the windows at the beautiful, shimmering waters of various lakes or rivers, the snowcapped peaks of tall mountains, and peaceful, serene valleys. But always in the back of their mind is the thought of an eventual station or point of disembarking. In fact, so intent are they on this station that they don't reap great benefits from the trip. It was evident from the way Hastings wrote that the dream was the trip of life, and we should not concentrate so much on the final destination, or station, that we miss the great joys along the way.

I have discovered in my life, as a result of substituting for teachers, the greatest joy is working with young people in an academic situation. On my journey, I have gained profound experience as a military communicator in the White House for the president. After my military service, I was able to complete my schooling (but my education continues on a daily basis) with the help of the GI Bill. Called into the preaching ministry, I completed a master of divinity degree at Southwestern Baptist Theological Seminary in Fort Worth, Texas. I have pastored small churches in Ida, Gainesville, Sherman, and Terrell, Texas. It also has been my privilege to be an interim pastor at several churches in East Texas. When God led me into public school teaching, I was flabbergasted. However, I learned a lesson from Elijah—wherever God leads you is where you need to go—be it Cherith, Zarephath, or public education. I have only just begun, and the joys are already tremendous.

Sondra was already teaching in Terrell, and I am teaching in Terrell. Matthew and Meredith are students in Terrell schools. I am teaching sixth grade social studies in the middle school.

What experiences does God have in store for us in the days to come? Like the kids, I can hardly wait to see what happens!

November 15, 1986

I am at the Hilton in Austin with John Griffin and Casey Wiley, two of the boys from our student council at Terrell Middle School. They are fine young people, and I enjoy them. Sometimes they puzzle me—and offend me with politeness. They answer my questions with a "yes, sir" or "no, sir" as if I were some dignitary with whom they are not familiar. I am not a dignitary. I'm just the student council cosponsor.

I'm the teacher in whose class one of these boys would set the clock on the wall ahead a few minutes ahead in hopes I would end class early. Perhaps it's just the generation gap—or perhaps I can't really be as much a part of their world as I want to be.

June 10, 1987

Sondra and the kids are at Falls Creek, Oklahoma. It's been very quiet around here this week. School and the upcoming EXCET test have kept me busy enough not to get too lonely. It has been a quiet existence.

The Homecoming

"Slick."

Joseph Evans blue eyes watched the road with apprehension. The last thing he wanted was for them to get stuck on a lonesome Texas highway in the dead of winter. Near the crest of the hill, when he felt the rear wheels of the car spin for half a second, he experienced a flash of the unreasonable irritability that had been plaguing him recently.

"Good thing it didn't snow more than an inch or two," he said grimly. "We'd be in trouble if it had." His wife was driving. She often did so he could make notes for a sermon or catch up on his endless correspondence by dictating into the tape recorder he had built into the car. He put his left arm on the back of the velour seat and tried to relax.

Virginia Evans looked out at the woods and fields, gleaming in the morning sunlight.

"It's pretty, though, and Christmassy. We haven't had a white Christmas like this in years."

He gave her an amused and affectionate glance. "You always see the best side of things, don't you?"

"Well, after hearing you urge umpteen congregations to do precisely that ..."

Joseph Evans smiled, and some of the lines of tension and fatigue went out of his face. "Remember the deal we made twenty years ago?" he said. "I'd do the preaching— and you'd do the practicing."

Her mouth curved in that familiar grin. "I remember."

They came to a crossroads, and he found that after all these years, he still remembered the sign: *Ida, 7 miles.*

He asked, "How's the time?"

She glanced at the diamond watch on her wrist, his present to her this year. "A little after ten."

He leaned forward and switched on the radio. In a moment, his own voice, strong and resonant, filled the car, preaching a Christmas sermon prepared and recorded weeks earlier. He listened to a sentence or two, then smiled sheepishly and turned it off.

"Just wanted to hear how I sounded."

"You sound fine," Virginia said. "You always do."

They passed a farmhouse, the new snow sparkling like diamonds on the roof, the Christmas wreath gay against the front door. A six-foot piñon pine in the front yard was trimmed with lights, unlit in the daytime.

"Who lived there?" he asked. "Petersen, wasn't it? No, Johannsen."

"That's right," his wife said. "Ted Johannsen. Remember the night he made you hold the lantern while the calf was born?"

"Do I ever." He rubbed his forehead wearily. "About this new television proposition, Virginia. What do you think?

It would be an extra load, I know. But I'd be reaching an enormous audience. The biggest ..."

She put her hand on his arm. "Darling, its Christmas Day. Can't we talk about it later?"

"Why, sure," he said, but something within him was offended all the same. The television proposal was important. Why, in fifteen minutes, he could reach ten times as many people as Saint Paul had reached in a lifetime. "How many people did the Ida church hold? About eighty, wasn't it?"

"Ministerially speaking," Virginia said. That sly smile showing her recognition of his habit of slight exaggeration with numbers. "Sixty-five to be exact."

"Sixty-five!" He gave a rueful laugh. "Quite a change of pace."

It was years since he had preached in anything but large metropolitan churches. The Ida church, in the North Central Texas countryside, had been the beginning. Now, on Christmas morning, he was going back, coming home. Back for an hour or two, to stand in the little pulpit where he had preached his first hesitant, fumbling sermon twenty years ago.

He let his head fall back against the seat and closed his eyes.

The decision to go back had not been his, really; it had been Virginia's. She handled all his appointments, screening the innumerable invitations to preach or speak. A month ago, she had come to him. There was a request, she said, for him to go back to Ida and preach a sermon on Christmas morning.

"Ida?" He had said, incredulous. "What about that Austin invitation?" He had been asked to a congregation that would, he knew, include state representatives, senators, and maybe even the governor.

"We haven't answered it, yet," she said. "We could drive to Ida on Christmas morning if we got up early enough."

He stared at her. "You mean, you think we ought to go back there?"

She had looked at him calmly. "That's up to you, Joe."

Still, he knew what she wanted him to say. *Making such a decision was not so hard at the moment,* he thought wearily; *not resenting it afterward was the difficult part.* Maybe it would not be so bad. The church would be horribly overcrowded, the congregation would be mostly farmers, but …

The car stopped. He opened his eyes.

They were at the church, all right. There it sat, by the side of the road where the road curved ever so slightly, just as it always had. If anything, it looked smaller than he had remembered. Around it, the fields stretched away, white and unbroken, to the neighboring farmhouses. There were no cars, there was no crowd, no sign of anyone. The church was shuttered and silent.

He looked at Virginia, bewildered. She did not seem surprised. She pushed open the car door.

"Let's go inside, shall we? I still have a key."

Once out of the car, he donned his black overcoat, and Virginia put on her high-collared navy Melton. He slammed the car door with a bang. The sound was almost as jolting as a blaring trumpet in the morning stillness.

Their footsteps crunched in the cold, solidly packed snow. When he put the key in the lock, it went in smoothly, but the door groaned and shuddered when he pushed it, as if it had been swollen in the last rainstorm and then frozen.

Inside, the church was cold. Standing in the icy gloom, he could see his breath steam in the gray light.

He said, and his voice sounded strange, "Where is everybody? You said there was a request …"

"There was a request," Virginia said. "From me."

She moved forward slowly until she was standing by the pulpit. "Joe, the finest sermon I ever heard you preach was right here in this church. It was your first Christmas sermon. We hadn't been married long. You didn't know that our first baby was on the way, but I did. Maybe that's why I remember so well what you said.

"You said that God had tried every way possible to get through to people. He tried prophets and miracles and revelations, and nothing worked. So then he said, 'I'll send them something that can't fail to understand. I'll send them the simplest and yet the most wonderful thing in all my creation. I'll send them a baby.' Do you remember that?"

He nodded wordlessly.

"Well, I heard that they had no minister here now, so I knew they wouldn't be having a service this morning. And I thought, well, I thought it might be good for … for both of us, if you could preach that sermon again. Right here, where your ministry began. I just thought …"

He knew what she meant. He knew what she was trying to tell him, although she was too loyal and too kind to say it in words. She was trying to say that he had gotten away from the sources of his strength. That as success had come to him, as his reputation had grown larger, some things in him had become smaller ... the selflessness, the humility ... the most important things of all.

He stood there, silent, seeing himself with a terrifying clarity: the pride, the ambition, the hunger for larger and larger audiences ... not for the glory of God but for the glory of Joe Evans.

He clenched his fists, feeling panic grip him, a sense of terror and guilt unlike anything he had ever felt, and yet there was the beginning of a feeling of comfort. Had he not preached for the past twenty years that one sometimes had to know there was a problem, and that this knowledge, in whatever way God chose to reveal it, was a beginning step in solving the problem?

Almost as though in an absentminded trance, he found himself wandering toward the back room he had known as his office. This place had also served as the church workroom. He recognized that some changes had been made. The last minister—whoever he had been—no longer needed to go downstairs to the boiler room to heat the church.

He felt comfortable in this office, even after twenty years. There was a familiarity to it, a sense of comfort, déjà vu, as though twenty years of time had vanished. He remembered that he had called this office his room of remembrance. It was here that he had communed with God every day back in the days when he remembered to consult God for advice about how even the most insignificant thing should be done.

Abruptly, he stripped off his overcoat, tossed it across the back of the chair. He rushed out and took both of Virginia's hands. He heard himself laugh, an eager, boyish laugh.

"We'll do it! We'll do it just the way we used to! You open the shutters—that was your job, remember? I'll sweep out the dust and heat up the old place. We'll have a Christmas service just for the two of us. I'll preach that sermon, all for you!"

She turned quickly to the nearest window, raised it, begun fumbling with the latch that held the shutters. He busied himself, turning the heat on and reminiscing about the many memories he had of this special place. It was only last year his wife had given him a painting by the talented young artist Kyle Wood done from a photograph of the church.

In the sanctuary, he heard a sound that made him pause. Virginia was trying to play "Break Thou the Bread of Life" on the old pump organ.

"Ring the bell too!" he shouted. "We might as well do the job right! You know I always said there was no sadder sight or thought than having a bell and not ringing it."

He made her laugh.

A moment later, from just outside the front door of the church, the bell began to ring. Its tone was as clear and resonant as ever, and the thought brought back a flood of memories: the baptisms, burials, Sunday dinners at the old farmhouses, and the honesty, brusqueness, and simple goodness of the people. He remembered one Christmas celebration when Matthew, their three-year-old son, had approached him and in a loud voice had said, "Daddy, can I have some beer?" Immediately he knew the boys who had put Matthew up to asking that question, and when he approached them, they had responded laughingly, "We said root beer."

He stood, listening, until the bell was silent. Then he came back into the sanctuary. The church was a blaze of sunlight. Where the window glass was clear, millions of dust notes whirled and danced; where there were panes of stained glass, the rays fell on the old floor in pools of ruby and amethyst.

Virginia was standing at the church door.

"Joseph," she said softly, "come here."

He walked over and stood beside her. After the darkness of the back room, the sun on the snow was so bright that he could not see anything.

"Look," she said in a whisper. "They're coming."

Cupping his hands round his eyes, he stared out across the glistening whiteness, and he saw that she was right. Parishioners were coming—across the fields, down the roads, some on foot, others in cars. They were coming, he knew, not to hear him, not to hear any particular preacher however well he might preach. They were coming because it was Christmas Day, and this was their church, and its bell was calling them. They were coming because they wanted someone to give them the Ancient Message, to tell them the Good News.

He stood with his arm around his wife's shoulders and with overflowing happiness in his heart.

"Merry Christmas," he said. "Merry Christmas to you. Happy birthday to him, and welcome home to me."

June 27, 1988

Sondra and the kids are on another church-sponsored trip. This time they are ministering in various nursing homes in San Antonio, and other points between there and here. They've been gone since Friday.

Today, the only human voices I heard were disappointing. This afternoon, someone called claiming to be three-and-a half-years-old and had learned how to dial the phone. When I asked if he had learned how to hang up, he had a rather perverse suggestion for me.

Then while I was umpiring tonight, the only voices I heard were the voices of fellow church members in the stands who were making fun of my calls. I'd really rather not be behind the plate when their kids are playing, but I have no control over that. It's eleven o'clock—time for sleep.

Adventures in Portugal and Spain

June 9, 2000

I have just returned from a brisk walk I took in Bem Pasta, Pastor Norman Harrell's neighborhood in Portimão, Portugal. Carolyn Porter, Kathy McCoulskey, and I have been in Portimão since Wednesday, May 31. Carolyn and Kathy are staying with Rebecca Porter, Carolyn's daughter, in her apartment, and I am staying in Pastor Norman's house, Villa Bempost, Portia.

The walk I enjoyed very much. Off in the distance, I could see hills. Nearer I could see an airport landing strip. Also, I saw a school where children were playing in the schoolyard. School is still in session here. We've been out of school for two weeks now.

We're here on a mission trip at Norman's invitation. We are teaching English as a Second Language (ESL) to interested Portuguese students. We hope to share witness with them. The Portuguese people are very friendly (I speak of those who are in the Portuguese-speaking church). English church members are also friendly, but they are a little restrained or reserved.

There actually is a settlement of English-speaking people from England who have lived here for years. They have not learned to speak Portuguese. Their services are held in the church on Sunday mornings.

Services for Moldavians, of which there is a sizeable segment of workers, are held at four on Sunday afternoon, and the Portuguese services are held at six on Sunday evening. The church has started a new ministry in a building about a block from here. Called La Pointe (The Bridge), this ministry includes serving coffee, conversation with inquirers, childcare, etc. The Bridge is actually an apartment building with commercial shops occupying the bottom two floors.

October 6, 2000

We departed, after picking up the ladies, for a little Saturday side trip to Spain. We stopped in the town of Lupe to get Spanish money, pesetas, at an ATM.

Just a little distance from Seville, to the northwest, are the ruins of an old Roman town called Italica. Started by Scipio in 206 BC as a fortress for Roman soldiers in their war against the Carthaginians, Italica became a thriving town. I'm anxious to see how the video looks. I am carrying an RCA video camera, and trying to operate it is a challenge. I saw some of the corridors of the coliseum as well as the main seating area and the entertainment area.

From there, we went to Seville. Lunch at a sidewalk café was enjoyable, and we soaked up the atmosphere. Then we went to a very large cathedral. The inside of the cathedral is the largest in the world. In the cathedral, there was an area dedicated to Christopher Columbus. There is a sarcophagus surrounded on four corners by Spanish kings. Inside the sarcophagus are, supposedly, the remains of Christopher Columbus.

We decided to go tour the Galindo Tower (name may be incorrect). We walked up a curving incline to the thirty-fifth level, and after catching our breath, looked out over the city. Would you believe the video camera has already lost battery power? It is a very beautiful city. Some areas of the city have pedestrian walkways and shopping areas.

After descending the tower, we went to the Alcazar Palace. The Moorish architecture is quite attractive with its angles and color schemes, and the gardens (*jardines*) are beautiful and breathtaking. The scent of apricots and oranges is delightful, but the fruit on the trees was beginning to become overripe.

The group got separated from me for a while, but I found them the second time I went to the exit. We arrived back at Norman's house in Portimão about 11:30 tired, but very satisfied with the activities of the day.

June 17, 2000

I am riding a bus on the way from Portimão, in southern Portugal, near the Mediterranean, to Lisbon. Sitting next to me is a young Portuguese man. Nelson has been in

Portimão for three days, but he is on his way back to Lisbon (*Lisboa*) to take exams to enter the university. He plans to become a PE teacher. He is very nice and makes an effort to talk with me. Nelson read my *testimunho pessoal* (personal testimony) for me in Portuguese and corrected some of my words. I asked him if he believes in God, and he said "Oh, yes! *Voce cre em Deus*?" We had a good conversation—some in Portuguese, some in Spanish, and some in English.

After arriving in Lisbon, we took a taxi to the Belem area. There we met Andy and Susan, and they have really been great hosts today. We have seen *Jerónimos Monasterio,* which was built in honor of Vasco da Gama, and in which is the tomb (sarcophagus) of da Gama. Building of the *monasterio* was paid for by funds that came to Portugal from da Gama's establishment of trade with India.

I have charged the video battery and am hoping the quality of my video is good enough for me to play for students in my sixth grade classes.

Across the street from the monastery is a large park where children from schools all over Lisbon participated in *Marche de Infantes* (the annual Children's Day activities in the city). Exciting music and cute kids made this enjoyable.

We also saw an old fort, the Tower of Belem, which was used for several purposes. It provided protection for the city from invasion by sea. It was also used as a place for prisoners during the Inquisition. Prisoners would be placed in holding areas beneath the floor and overhead gates with bars three or four inches apart would be closed and locked. When the tides rose at night, prisoners usually drowned. According to our guide, those who didn't drown were considered to be innocent and were released.

The monument to Portuguese explorers was very impressive. Prince Henry, Vasco da Gama, Pedro Nunez, Pedro Cabral, and Christopher Columbus were among those depicted. It was a very large work.

Tomorrow, we shall attend church, and there will be more sights to see. The red splotches on my lower legs are bothersome, but maybe they will abate overnight.

June 18, 2000

We went to church, which started at 11:30 at the International Baptist Church of Lisbon— on the first floor of the *Terceira Igreja Evangelica Baptist de Lisbon* on *Rua Filipe Folque.*

The sound of the choir downstairs, singing in Portuguese, was forceful and exciting. Our church had mostly Africans from different English-speaking countries in Africa (Kenya, South Africa, Nigeria, etc.) but also an English-speaking lady from Germany. The song leader was Portuguese, but he spoke excellent English. After dismissal, members of the Portuguese church mingled in the street for at least half an hour, hugging each other and having fellowship. It was quite an encouraging sight.

After lunch, we did some more sightseeing beginning at an old castle, *Castle de São Jorge* (St. George Castle). My vertigo almost got the best of me. I don't understand what I refer to as selective vertigo. Sometimes it just happens, and at other times, I can be in a very high location and not be bothered at all. Today, I walked up the outer stairway to get to the higher parts of the castle. When I came to go back down that outer stairway (no outer rail) I froze. I couldn't move. I broke out in perspiration. After what seemed like an hour, I managed to get back down.

Lisbon is a beautiful, old city. I'd love to spend more time here. My curiosity almost got the best of me. On the ride up to the castle, which is in an older section of the city, I noticed a man urinating against the wall of a building in full view of other people. Those people didn't seem fazed by his activities at all. When I asked Pastor Norman about that, he said, "It's a common occurrence here. We do have public restrooms, but a person has to pay to use the facilities. Those who think they can't pay just relieve themselves as discreetly as they can in public. It's no big deal."

A street guitarist, Pedro Godinho, was playing his guitar in one of the level places at the castle. I bought his CD and am playing it now as I write this. It sets a *saudade* or relaxing and calmly sad mood.

There is a little nine-year-old boy in Portimão named Amadeus. He has dancing brown eyes and an impish grin. He seems to appear and disappear with ease. Amadeus speaks both Portuguese and Spanish with a little English thrown in. Amadeus and his friend, Frederico, who lives in Cade Praia, do not know Jesus personally. They are lost! Will someone find Amadeus? Doesn't his name mean love of God? Then, will someone find Frederico?

June 26, 2000

The drive up to *Castelo Branco* was very enjoyable. We drove in a caravan of four vans (rented) and one car.

After Sunday's services and the fellowship with both churches (English and Portuguese), I was still feeling good. Brother Ernie McCoulskey preached the morning English service, and I preached the evening Portuguese service with Marcos Melo as interpreter. I preached "If We Love God" (1 John 5:1–5), my favorite sermon to preach, and it was well received. I concluded the sermon using their Portuguese language.

We drove through the *Alantico* into some mountains in which *Castelo Branco* is located. Our hotel, *Colino do Castelo*, is near the top of the highest hill in the city. From the hotel, and the castle walls on a little rising above the hotel, all of the city can be seen.

We are here to help during the First Annual Iberian Mission meetings. Some are working with preschoolers (keeping them so that parents can attend meetings). Sondra and several others are working with grades 1–6 on SMAK (Summer Music Activities for Kids); others are working in a program for youth (teens who are missionary kids).

Sondra and the rest of our group from First Baptist of Terrell arrived in Portimão a few days ago. We spent a couple days in a hotel on the beach at Portimão. I had already been here for three weeks, and although I greatly enjoyed the hospitality of Norman and Geneva Harrell, I was ready to have my wife with me. One of the things

I was able to share with her was that the McDonald's in Portimão is affectionately called McNorman's by people of the church in honor of Norman Harrell, a frequent customer.

Here in *Castelo Branco*, I am a "floater," though I was originally assigned to youth. Also I am involved in "prayer walking," and I "float" in and out of the preschool (little toddlers) to relieve workers there.

In the morning, my group meets in the snack bar of the hotel. After Bible study, youth sub in the preschool department for an hour. They relieve Adult workers so those workers can have an hours' break. Then the youth go to recreation and then lunch at one. At 3:30, Bible study is followed by more recreation.

What is Missions? First, let me say what it isn't. It isn't some faceless, unknown person being sent to do God's work in a foreign land. Missions is real people, flesh and blood, with emotions and needs just as you and I have. We all need love—emotional, mental, and spiritual support—to know that someone cares.

Missions is the Bartlett family in Spain. They deal with being ostracized by the society into which they are thrust. They deal with being stared at or ignored because they are *extranjeros*—foreigners. They cope with being thought of as "evangelicals" in a society or culture that automatically thinks of Jehovah's Witnesses or Mormons when the word "evangelical" is spoken.

Perhaps they can cope because they receive love, emotional, mental, and spiritual support from those of us who really do care. The Bartletts are from the Bonham area and have two boys: Caleb is fifteen, and Corbin is eight. The Bartletts are serving in southern Spain, but they may start new work in the north of Spain where there are cities and suburbs with populations of two million people and no Baptist witnesses.

The Harrells in Portimão, Portugal, have a well-established work. *The Internacional Igreja de Portimão* (*25 de Abril*) has three congregations meeting in the same facility at different times. The English congregation meets at eleven on Sundays. The Moldavians meet at two in the afternoon. Sometimes they stay for the Sunday school at five, and the Portuguese congregation's worship service begins at six.

Each of the congregations has indigenous leadership in music with guitars and/or keyboards. The church also now has Rita and Antonio Magnani in leadership roles. In addition to leading music in the Portuguese services, Rita is the director of programs at The Pointe" in *Sede Praia*—a high-rise building near the church. "The Pointe" is a room in the bottom floor of the building that is being purchased by the church. Among the programs already started are Monday coffees from ten to noon, AA programs Monday evenings, and Ladies Day out on Wednesdays from ten to five. Ladies can leave their children at the Pointe while they are shopping. These programs are all in their beginning stages.

The ESL classes we taught for three weeks did establish some contacts on which the church can follow up. Continuing classes need to be taught on a regular basis.

Magnani, as he likes to be called, has been going to the church for about a year. He has been on staff for about two months. He and Rita, originally from Angola, met at the church after Rita moved to Portimão from northern Portugal and began going to the church. They were married about four months ago.

Since Marcos Melo, their seminary intern for four years, has graduated from seminary in Lisbon, he'll no longer be coming to Portimão twice a month. Magnani will handle the services in his place. Magnani is originally from Brazil. He speaks Portuguese and Italian, and he is learning English. Rita speaks Portuguese and French, and she is advanced in learning English. It should be exciting to see what God does with them. Portugal right now is "stony ground," but perhaps God will use these two to soften the soil. They are terrific missionaries.

Articles, Editorials, Essays, and Laments

Carl*

There are different ways to die and various types of death. Death is not just the absence of breathing or the cessation of brain activity. That is one type of death, physical death, the less serious type.

Another type of death exists, however: the loss of light and life within a body that still physically functions.

"Funeral services for Joshua Carl Turner will be held from the First Baptist Church in Terrell at 4:00 p.m. Friday, April 17, in Terrell. Carl died Wednesday, April 15, in Terrell." The obituary didn't say that Carl leveled a shotgun to the side of his head, pulled the trigger, and violently ended his own life. "He died," it said, as if he had peacefully gone to sleep never to awaken again.

Carl's death on April 15 concluded a process that began on a Wednesday night two years earlier when Carl's parents informed him of their impending separation and divorce. "It has nothing to do with you kids," they said. They wanted him to know they both loved him very much, but they no longer loved each other. Somehow thirteen-year-old Carl just couldn't understand.

From that night—when Carl came to our house to share the news and asked me what he could do to make them change their minds—Carl suffered excruciating emotional pain. He asked me to talk them out of their plans, and I tried. Unbeknownst to him, they had warned me beforehand about telling Carl and the other two kids about the divorce. They feared the effect it might have on Carl. I had already tried to persuade them to let God heal their wounds and save their marriage. "Too late," they said. "Too much has already happened."

I wanted to bear Carl's pain and relieve him of it entirely. But nothing I said or did could help him. I understood his pain because I had experienced similar pain as a child.

Carl used to confide some things to me that troubled him. We would talk about a few things he did, and how he didn't understand why he did them. "What's wrong with me?" he would say. I recognized his calls for help, and I tried to help him see himself as a good person, one much loved by me and others. He wanted his father's love, and his father wasn't around anymore. Now, Carl isn't around either. I never got to say good-bye. Am I doing that by writing this?

The divorce affected Carl severely. I helplessly watched him suffer as if both his parents had died and left him all alone. Divorce is a type of death, especially for those who constantly feel they have been rejected by the very people whose union in love brought them into this world. It can be a slow and agonizing death for those innocent ones who can't cope. Carl couldn't, and he died. Part of me died too. I wonder if he knows that. There are different ways to die and various types of death.

*Name changed to protect the privacy of this individual and his survivors.

The Honey and the Money

A jar of honey chanced to spill
Its contents on the windowsill
In many a viscous pool and rill.
The flies, attracted by the sweet,
Began so greedily to eat,
They smeared their fragile wings and feet.
With many a twitch and pull in vain
They gasped to get away again,
And died in aromatic pain.

The truth of this fable of Aesop's might have been said by Abraham Lincoln:
"One can catch more flies with honey than with vinegar."
It might also be stated in the following manner:
"What doth it profit a man if he gains
The whole world and loses his own soul?"
—Matthew 16:26a

In Texas, the jar of "honey money" has been spilled. It is called the lottery. Millions of dollars are available—just waiting for some lucky "super fly" to "catch the scent" and come get his nectar. Every few weeks, someone wins a lot of "honey money."

Of course, some chance or risk is involved. One must purchase a ticket, or a series of tickets, if he or she wants to increase the chances of winning. One can never tell when one might purchase the ticket that has those lucky numbers. And if he or she doesn't have the winning combination, so what? They'll get them next time. And even if they don't, it's all right because a good percentage of the state's profit will benefit public education, won't it?

"Some people approach every problem with an open mouth," Adlai Stevenson said.

Some years ago, before the November election dealing with the lottery issue, many Texas voters wondered how a lottery would benefit the state. Other states had tried a lottery and not really benefited from it the way the government representatives indicated they would. "How will a lottery help us when it hasn't helped them?"

Several Texas politicians approached this problem with an open mouth. Representative Ron Wilson of Houston, Bob Bullock, and Gib Lewis said it would be possible for the state to devote a small percentage of the profits from the lottery to help finance part of public education in Texas. Texans who heard these statements and wrote personal notes about them were astonished and amazed at the miracle of having heard something that, according to then Governor Ann Richards, never was said. The governor didn't say it for the record, but Wilson, Lewis, and Bullock did. After reading the January and September 1991 issues of *Texas Monthly,* issues in which the representatives were quoted as indicating public education would be partially funded by the lottery should voters approve it in the election, I wrote in my journal: *I'll believe it when I see it.*

However, whether or not lottery profits were ever to have been dedicated to public education is not really the issue. Can a society benefit when the government proposes a system to enhance the state's financial structure—and has a secondary feature of possibly being lucrative for a lucky few citizens?

By definition, a lottery is "a scheme for the distribution of prizes by lot or chance; a scheme by which prizes are distributed to the winners among those persons who have paid for a chance to win them, usually as determined by the numbers on tickets drawn at random."

The "flies" are swarming to little stores all over Texas. They are "smearing their fragile wings and feet" without realizing they are getting stuck. What will happen when they begin to experience the pain and "try to pull away in vain?"

Perhaps if Aesop were alive today, he would say, "Oh, foolish creatures that destroy themselves for transitory joy."

Lament for Parker

Anyone who has ever played in the snow as a child knows the pain of cold fingers and toes from remaining outside for too long. Our circulation reminds us that human anatomy is not designed to accommodate prolonged exposure to frigid temperatures, as the burning, stinging sensation brings tears and vows of never doing that again.

No matter what our age or the sources of our suffering, pain gets our attention. We can deny it or medicate it, ignore or tolerate it, but pain will try to have the last say. Whether emotional or physical, distancing ourselves from pain buys time, but not solutions.

In an essay from *The Clown in the Belfry*, Frederick Buechner said, "We are never more alive to life than when it hurts—never more aware of both of our own powerlessness to save ourselves and of at least the possibility of a power beyond ourselves to save us and heal us if we can only open ourselves to it."

Opening ourselves to pain is born of leaning into our emotions, our circumstances, our hurts, and our hopes, and thereby walking through our pain to the healing on the other side. If our singular goal is to simply eradicate pain, we miss the saving grace to be found within. Pain, particularly emotional pain, is often the seedbed of sanctified discontent, providing the inner momentum to move us out of ruts, damaging relationships, and destructive situations. Pain is always a catalyst for action. Corrie ten Boom said, "There is no pain so dark and fearsome that God cannot be found within it."

Parker was born in the year 1985, a time I call my time of discontent. Perhaps I should call it my time of "conflict" although it wasn't the only time I ever had conflict. In the spring of that year, I was asked if I would consider being a substitute for a teacher while she was out on maternity leave. I asked my church if they would consider allowing me to do so, and I got a resounding yes to the question. For a month, I substituted as an English teacher, and as I recall, we were reading *Pygmalion* by George Bernard Shaw. One of the students was a young man named Eric Bishop (later known as Jamie Foxx).

The conflict? I enjoyed this teaching so much that I began to question if that wasn't what God wanted me doing. How could he who had called me into the pastorate now be moving me to be a teacher? *God just doesn't do that,* I reasoned. For several months, this internal struggle almost consumed me. In August, the conflict became urgent. I was asked to take a teaching position just vacated by a veteran teacher. The school year would be starting in a week. *What would other people think if I resigned my church and became a full-time teacher?* God helped me see that it was more important for me to wonder what he would think if I didn't follow his leadership—even when it made no sense to me. After several months of contemplation, meditation, pain, and prayer, I yielded. While I was becoming a teacher, God was teaching me.

I became acquainted with Parker and his family because they attended the church we joined after I became a public school teacher. He was a baby who had an active and joyful life as a youngster. When he was twelve years old, Parker was in my social studies class. I began to notice some differences in Parker. Some of his joy was gone. He was becoming a little withdrawn and distant. When I approached his mom and stepdad with my concerns, they shared with me that Parker was sad because his mom had a certain type of cancer that would eventually be fatal. He was angry with God for allowing this to happen.

Though I tried several times to talk with Parker over the next two years, he wasn't ready to understand why his mom had to suffer so much. Though he was glad she could be medicated, the medicine zapped her of energy and vitality. After her death, Parker became even more withdrawn and sullen. A well-behaved student in the sixth grade, Parker began to have behavior problems at school.

His grandparents adopted him and tried to provide him with a loving and stable home environment. His anger, however, was still unabated. They thought sending him to the Agape School in Maryland would give him a fresh start. There, a professor of animal husbandry took a special interest in Parker. This professor, a good Christian man, selected Parker to work with him and his animals. They became good friends, and Parker was helped. However, Parker never lost the anger that kept building within him. Still searching, Parker joined the military. He was stationed in Afghanistan. Three times, the minesweeper he drove was partially destroyed by mines. Parker was the recipient of the Purple Heart for his heroism. He saw the horrors of war on a scale that most of us never experience. When he came home, he was still angry with God. He was still experiencing inner turmoil. Alcohol and other drugs were means of escape for him, but they never provided peace. His family and others loved him greatly, but they couldn't provide him with peace. Only God could do that, and Parker was still angry with God.

Earlier in this lament, I wrote that I knew something about Parker's pain. I could only write that from the viewpoint of one who saw Parker's pain, one who has experienced some type of pain in life, but not from the viewpoint of one who has experienced that very same pain. Only Parker knows exactly what that pain was like, and he couldn't express it in a way that gave him real relief.

On a Thursday morning, Parker ended his life and his constant battle with anger and pain. We who love him can't condemn him for what he did. We can only lament, and each of us does that in his or her own way.

JD Emard

"JD is your favorite person ever. Admit it! JD loves you! You know I'm your favorite."

These playful little messages, and others like them, gave me insight into the inner thoughts of a sixth-grade boy. JD Emard needed a lot of reassurance, as many people of all ages do, and I gave it to him.

JD was a precocious, mischievous, playful, restless, active boy, who couldn't sit still in a student desk for more than a few minutes at a time. Fortunately, in social studies, it was possible for a student to occasionally move about without being disruptive.

Jonathan was frequently a role player in various historical (sometimes hysterical) vignettes. As a fantastic Mark Anthony, he delivered a moving, not-quite-Shakespearean oration about Julius Caesar's death.

With his almost limitless supply of energy, JD got involved in extracurricular activities after leaving the sixth grade. He became involved in Community Theater in Rockwall. My wife and I went to see his performance. Of course, it was energetic! His older sister, of whom he was quite proud, sings quite well.

Jonathan was one of the searchers I wrote about earlier. Perhaps he found what he was searching for in the military.

The official military press release said: *Three Mountain Division soldiers were killed June 4 when they were engaged by enemy forces with small-arms fire and hand grenades while their unit was assaulting a building near*

Hawijah, Iraq … Spc Jonathan D. Emard was assigned to 1st Battalion, 87th Infantry Regiment, 1st Brigade Combat Team 10th Mountain Division, Fort Drum, New York.

There was, of course, an accompanying picture of Jonathan in his military gear. As I studied the picture, I didn't so much see the face of a twenty-year-old man as I did the face of a twelve-year-old in sixth grade at Wood Intermediate School in Terrell.

I find myself contemplating an oration or writing a lament for Jonathan's death. Jonathan's awards and decorations include the Purple Heart, the National Defense Service Medal, and the Combat Infantryman Badge. JD would have earned many more awards had he lived beyond his twentieth year. None of those awards or medals is as meaningful to us who love him as is the fact that we had his heart and he has ours forever.

Austria, Germany, Switzerland

July 26, 2007

> He will yet fill your mouth with laughter
> and your lips with shouts of joy.
> —Job 8:21

Our mouths were filled with laughter after we took off from Dallas/Fort Worth International Airport on Delta flight #1108 bound for Atlanta. Everyone was in a good mood. I am still in a good mood, but I lost my library book. We also had a three-hour delay in Atlanta. Our connecting flight was late, and there were mechanical difficulties with the air conditioning.

I talked with a young Austrian named Markus who was delightfully effervescent in personality. He wants to play in the National Basketball Association. Markus has been playing for a college team in Georgia. He's from an area forty-five minutes east of Vienna, near the Czech border.

July 27, 2007

The Hapsburgs ruled for 645 years—from the late 1200s to 1918. The Schönbrunn Palace was incredible. Seeing this magnificent palace really added some life to my historical view of the Hapsburgs. They came to Austria in 1273. They started an empire in 1278 and ruled until 1918. Touring Schönbrunn should be done in two days—not two hours.

July 28, 2007

On Saturday afternoon, we visited Mozart's first apartment in Vienna. He and his wife lived there for two and a half years. Before we started the tour, two of our ladies needed a restroom break. However, they couldn't get the WC door to open. Carolyn and Pat thought it was locked. When I looked at it, there was no keyhole!

How could it possibly be locked? I pushed the door, and it opened. Embarrassed, the ladies had not tried to push on the door. They had only pulled.

The tour was quite revealing and interesting, especially the erotic writings of Mozart. Pat saw one scene, and her opinion of Mozart changed.

July 29, 2007

I wonder if there is a way I can write a description of Vienna that is not confined by words, such as beautiful, exquisite, charming, exciting, intriguing, and historical. When we arrived at our hotel and finally got our room assignments settled, I was so tired. I wanted to rest for two hours. Others took a walking tour of the Ring, a circular route that connects to every part of Vienna. Later, we took a bus tour around the Ring.

What is said to be the largest Ferris wheel in Europe is just a few blocks from our hotel, but I don't think time to ride it is allowed in our schedule. I don't think I can persuade Sondra to go up on it anyway. I remember seeing this Ferris wheel on one of the Joseph Cotten-Orson Welles movies.

Last night, our group went to one of the famous restaurants in Vienna, which makes and serves its own wine. Several members of our group became a little consternated by the idea of a Baptist group of travelers being served wine. I am not upset with them, but I am a bit amused. What did they expect from a place whose name description includes the words *wine garden*?

My wife and I discreetly poured the wine into a flowerpot in the outdoor garden area. That probably has happened before. It looks like a very healthy plant!

July 29, 2007

We departed Vienna on a boat cruise on the Danube from Dernsley to Melk—a two-and-one-half hour cruise. Parts of the Danube were beautiful—and scenes on the shores were eye-catching. The prerecorded information broadcast over a series of speakers was in German, English, French, Spanish, and Japanese. Before the cruise, we walked through the town. Arduous was the ascent into the town, and the descent was less of a problem. Donna's broken foot gave her some trouble, but she was a champion—not a victim.

After we left *Das Boot* at Melk (with Oreos), we briefly toured the beautifully ornate abbey. In Salzburg, we stayed at the Renaissance Marriott Hotel.

On Monday night, we went to the St. Peter's Restaurant (continually operating since 803 when Charlemagne was a guest). We heard and saw a terrific presentation of some of Mozart's music. Salzburg was where he was born. Both houses were in good condition.

At intermission, Julie went to the WC. She returned just as the program was resuming, and she walked in at the same time that the male performer came in. She had quite an effective entrance and earned a round of applause.

Salzburg is also quite an international city about which I would like to learn more. An independent state for quite a time, it did not become a part of Austria until the early 1800s.

August 1, 2007

This morning, we left Salzburg bound for Munich (*München*) for a city tour and shopping spree before continuing on for *Oberammergau*. I am thinking of John Porter's hand. He accidentally poured hot coffee on his right hand yesterday morning at the Renaissance Hotel. We stuck his hand in a bowl of cold water and put ice on it. He was in agony for a little while. One of our group members, a nurse, recommended a certain type of cream to rub on it and a bandage to cover the burn. Later as we were walking around at Eagle's Nest (Hitler's retreat), he seemed to not be experiencing quite as much pain. He was trying to play it down, but I know it was a serious burn.

Eagles Nest provoked or evoked some serious feelings in me. One of the ladies in our group was a resident of Poland as a child when the German blitzkrieg occurred. I wondered what she was thinking as she stood on that peak, looking at the cross that overlooked Hitler's mountain retreat. The look on her face defied my descriptive ability. Was it the pain from suppressed memories that were revived after years of dormancy? Was it the sadness from thinking about what might have been if Hitler had not come to power? Was she thinking of the family members who might have lived? Was she thinking of what descendants might have come had those people lived? Was there the finality of realizing that Hitler is gone—and she is still alive? Was she seeing evil in this place? How would I feel—and what would I think—if I were her?

At Eagle's Nest, we encountered a long, wide tunnel with reinforced steel doors. A large vehicle could be driven in this tunnel. At the end of the tunnel, there was an airshaft (maybe three inches wide by four feet long). We turned right into a short, wide hallway. The elevator was about twelve feet wide and eighteen feet deep. We were crammed into the car so tightly that we pressed against each other. Fortunately, most of our group had showered and cleaned up before the trip. A few people from other groups didn't have such good hygiene. They were no problem in the tunnel, which was about twenty degrees cooler than it was outside. The elevator was a different story. The ride only took about three minutes to go up to the top (sixty floors if the elevator indicator was correct).

August 1, 2007

Hitler didn't use this as a living area. It was used as a place for foreign dignitaries (Mussolini was there twice) to visit and confer. Eva Braun liked the place much more than Hitler did. An evil man had the road and house built in thirteen months (1937–8), but the place itself isn't evil (except for the prices in the restaurant).

I have some answers to my questions about the lady at Eagles Nest. Gladys said she felt very sick at first. She had to sit down after leaving the elevator, which very much reminded her of one of those railroad cars. Though she is not Jewish, she reminded us that the Nazis killed others. As she was sickened and had to sit down, it reminded her of the time she toured Auschwitz. Her uncle, an American, was gassed and burned there. Her father, also an American, was also in Auschwitz, but he escaped.

"As I stood facing the Cross," Gladys said, "I felt a real peace." After she told me this, I thought about how often the Cross has that effect on people. Before experiencing the Cross, we are in torment, but after accepting the one sacrificed there, we are at peace.

We were at the conclusion of our tour of Innsbruck when we had this conversation.

At 8:30, we departed on a day trip to Innsbruck, Austria, the site of the 1964 and 1978 Winter Olympics. We stopped for several picture-taking opportunities. Donna wasn't too keen on having pictures taken because she had burned her hair with her curling iron. Her thin gray hair in the front now has a brown tinge to it.

Our Innsbruck guide, Angelica, was quite informative. Probably our best guide was Mannfred in Salzburg. He was a professor, judge, and tour guide.

August 2, 2007

Inn is the name of the river that runs through Innsbruck, and it is the inspiration for the name.

Oberammergau is a beautiful town of around 4,500 people. I am struck by the beauty of the flowers in the window boxes. I like it.

Our Collette trip manager just got on the bus intercom and said, "Better to fart (fahrt) and bear the shame than not to fahrt and bear the pain." I'm wondering if he has just done what he was talking about.

The Wittelsbach Hotel is very old, but it is maintained well. It has a quaint charm. Walking through the city was a very serene and relaxing experience. The town is almost immaculately clean! Greg says it is a wealthy town. Most houses are large and have price tags of about 1.25 million Euros. Hundred-year mortgages are common. Two or three generations of a family may live in the same house.

The Passion Play occurs here every ten years; the next one will be in 2010. Almost every person living in

Oberammergau takes part. A year before the play, men stop shaving in order to grow their beards for whatever characters they will portray. Some traditions are worth maintaining!

From Oberammergau, we are motoring by bus to Titisee (Black Forest) by way of Lindau (and having lunch in Lindau). From a distance, we saw two castles constructed by Leopold I and Leopold II (Hohenswanstein and Neuschwanstein). Interesting stories are connected with each.

First we saw Wieskirche (White Church), which also has an interesting history. Wieskirche began after a couple was searching through an attic on property left to them by deceased relatives. There they found several old statues—one of which was of Christ and consisted of body parts from different statues—giving the statue an unusual form. This statue was later used in a very small chapel where worship occurred. One morning, the man came excitedly into his house and proclaimed, "The statue is crying." When this was reported to the bishop, it was decided that a larger church should be built and the statue would be the centerpiece backdrop. Several instances of the statue "crying" have been reported.

We are traveling through an agricultural region of Germany. There is a large lake on the left, Lake Constance, and a very large vineyard on the right. We've also passed apple, plum, date, and pear orchards. Fruit is plentiful, apparently, in this part of the world.

Historical and social note: In Germany, twelve Euros are placed in an account for each newborn baby. On that baby's birthday each year until the age of eighteen, the government places twelve more Euros in that account. Germans are good at saving.

I am anxious to see the Black Forest.

August 3, 2007

We saw very little of the Black Forest. I had hoped we would get to go on some of the walking paths so we could spend a few minutes celebrating her birthday by ourselves. However, we were only there for the night, and we had an obligatory presentation to attend in a shop. We purchased a grandfather clock to be shipped home. Also, I bought some Hummel figurines for Sondra, and I will try to hide them until Christmas. The figurines are little musicians.

August 4, 2007

We have just crossed the border from Germany into Switzerland at Basel. Switzerland is a neutral country. Every male citizen of Switzerland is obligated to serve eighteen months in the military. Females have a choice. Every Swiss man is expected to be proficient with firearms. It is very difficult to become a naturalized citizen of Switzerland. People from other countries are allowed to come here to work, but they must leave Switzerland one month of the year. They reapply for permission to enter and work each year. Political divisions in Switzerland are called cantons (*Kantons*), and there are twenty-three of them. Austria and Germany have states.

Before we left this morning, I observed a German boy who was seven or eight years old. He was doing some exercises on a bar in the playground. Since it had rained earlier, the bar was wet. The enterprising young boy simply used the bottom of his blue T-shirt to dry off the bar. I told him, mostly by using signs, that he was using his head (good thinking), and he smiled and said *"Danke Schoen*, sir." That was refreshing for me.

Pam C. was very considerate of Sondra this morning (she usually is) and gave her a plastic bag in case she gets nauseous in the back of the bus. It is a feminine hygiene bag.

At eleven, we arrived at Bern, the capital of Switzerland. Which has a population of 40,000 people. We did not stop at the Bear Platz as we were supposed to do— disappointing. However, the *Château de Chillon* was well worth the wait to see. On the outskirts of Micheaux, the Château is actually on an island also called Chillon. The Savoy family (counts and dukes) had it built in the mid-thirteenth century. More than 750 years old, the castle has been in the hands of the Savoy family, the French (200 years), and Savoy family again. All the original fourteen toilets are positioned on the lakeside of the castle for strategic reasons. One member of the Savoy family was a count, a duke, and then pope (when there were three popes ruling). He resigned when unification under one pope in Rome took place. He retired to one of his castles (there were twenty-five of them) as he put it "to eat." I think I understand as we have eaten very well on this trip.

August 4, 2007

Slept until 6:15 after going to bed at ten o'clock. In Vermaat we are staying at the Schweizerhof Hotel (a Seiler Hotel). It is a five-star hotel (more than we are used to). From Tosch we came by train because automobiles powered by petrol are not allowed in Vermaat. The bus ride to Tosch was exciting because of the combination of narrow twisting roads and altitude. Some of the views, however, were magnificent.

Greg's judgment in threatening to grab the wheel and crash through the barrier was probably faulty. Some people were actually scared. I didn't pay too much attention to Greg since I was praying for the bus driver (Karl) at the time. I was reminded about times when Ross Perry (my earthly father) would drive around those West Virginia mountain curves at what seemed like a high rate of speed when I was five or six. He would always take the mountain curve too fast right before driving off the right side of the road onto a dirt road that spiraled down the mountain toward his sister Gaye's house. Did I mention he would be drinking at the time? Did I mention I was prone to carsickness? I wonder if there was a connection.

Since I am writing this, it is quite evident that Karl got us to Tosch in good health physically and mentally. James Dickerson did pull Greg aside for a bit of a serious talk.

We transferred to the train that brought us up to Vermaat in about fifteen minutes. There were more spectacular views. I hope Sondra's camera wasn't shaking too much as she took the pictures. I faced her so I could see where we were going—and she could see where we had been.

The Matterhorn

I have been to the mountaintop. We have pictures to prove it. We met a Japanese couple on the log train up to *Gornergrat* (Matterhorn). Their names were Moshi and Ai. He is studying finance, and she is studying languages at the University of Georgia. Talking with them was really a delight.

The chapel near the top of the hill was really "High Church." We had our picture taken with Moshi and Ai. We also had our pictures taken yesterday with James and Pat and with Benny and Bella (two large Saint Bernards).

Grandfather Pauley would really have loved the Swiss Alps. I couldn't help but think of him today as we have seen all these sights. In his later years, he dreamed of taking the gospel to Brazil, Switzerland, and China. He never went to any of those places, of course, except within the confines of his mind. But I have now been to two of those places. Maybe I somehow have taken him with me.

Before I stop writing about Vermaat, I want to include one tidbit of information about Brent and Pam. Brent and Pam went to the spa, and there was an outside area to relax, tan, etc. They didn't realize it was an area where nudity was accepted. They were there several hours.

Pam asked, "Why would they want to tan *that*?"

I didn't ask what *that* was, but Pam explained that some missionaries in Africa refer to them as "mud flaps."

August 5, 2007

Today we left Vermaat bound for Lucerne with a little side trip to Interlaken. Karl stopped at a high-elevation mountain pull-off, and our Mercedes-Benz bus took up all the available space. We took pictures of some spectacular scenes. A couple of ladies stayed on the bus because they were queasy. Pam and Sondra have some trouble with high, narrow spaces that make it appear as though you might drop in on someone unexpectedly).

We stopped at Marmot for forty-five minutes. That is not its real name. I just called it that because this little place actually has marmots in large enclosures (also a white owl and a raccoon).

We ate a late lunch at BeBe's Restaurant. Several group members thought BeBe was ADD because he was a dynamo who never slowed down. He did some unusual things like wearing "cow pants," and wearing an udder cap on his head and then in an erogenous zone. Perhaps he was having gender issues. He is a fun-loving bodybuilder.

We saw the Grand Hotel and the field where windsurfers land.

We arrived at the Astoria Hotel in Lucerne at 5:30 after seeing the statue of a dying lion. City fathers commissioned the statue to honor members of the elite Swiss Guard who were killed while fighting to protect the King Louis XVI and Marie Antoinette. After the artist finished, he was not paid the full amount promised him. He re-erected his scaffolding and put finishing touches on his masterpiece. He changed the background outline in which the lion was sculpted to look like a pig's head.

August 6, 2007

Sondra, Pam, and Pat were glad to get off the winding roads of the mountains. As for me, I would like to have spent more time on the ground and less time on the bus.

Last night we slept in room 3601 of the Astoria Hotel. There is a full-length mirror on the wall opposite the window. When I awoke at six for a bathroom visit, I looked at the mirror, thinking I was facing the window. Disoriented, I walked toward the window, expecting to find the bathroom. Fortunately, I was able to navigate toward the right place. Had the window been open, someone down below could have been showered with an unexpected downfall.

We took a cruise on Lake Lucerne today. Actually I am not sure a one-hour boat ride qualifies as a "cruise," but "cruise" sure sounds better than a "one-hour boat ride."

The lake is the largest lake entirely within the borders of Switzerland. Scenic is probably an understatement when describing this lake and its shores.

Genaro, a friendly waiter from Bolivia, is on my mind tonight. I wonder if he is a Christian. He's probably a Roman Catholic. He says he likes Switzerland and enjoys working here. It seems as if employees in the restaurant are not accustomed to having conversations with guests.

Wh*at does God have in mind for him?* I asked him that question, and he replied that he really didn't know, but he's going on his one month's holiday soon and may know the answer if he is allowed to come back to Switzerland. You see, foreign workers in Switzerland must take their holiday and leave the country. They have to reapply for permission to come back into the country and resume their old job.

August 7, 2007

Sondra and I had a mix-up at the airport. While I went to the tax refund window, she went on to Gate E27 where I was to meet her.

When I got to the security checkpoint, I didn't have my boarding pass. Sondra had both boarding passes, and she had already checked through the security checkpoint. I said, "My wife has my boarding pass, and she has already gone through to Gate E27."

She said, "Sir, I am not supposed to allow anyone past this point without a boarding pass. Go on, but don't ever do this again!"

I passed through and went on to gate E27.

Sondra, realizing that I did not have my boarding pass, had gone back to the security checkpoint with Greg Willets, our tour manager. Security sent them to Terminal A (where people are supposed to go when they don't have boarding passes at the security checkpoint). Of course, I wasn't there. I was at Gate E27, wondering where Sondra and Greg had gone. I wasn't worried. They were being paged, and I had no doubt they would return soon.

In the meantime, I was being paged, but I couldn't hear the page. Apparently the page didn't reach our terminal. My page for Sondra apparently didn't reach where she had been sent. Sondra arrived back as we were boarding. However, we still had half an hour before takeoff. Sondra wouldn't have known to come back to the departure terminal if another tour manager hadn't found her and let her know I was at the terminal. Our own tour manager had left her to be sure he wouldn't miss the plane. Meanwhile, I had purchased each of us a soft drink and pastry, knowing she would need a little refreshment. Those two soft drinks and pastries cost more than the tax refund I had gotten.

This was not the only excitement in the past two days. While part of the group was on Mount Pilatus yesterday, one of the gondola support lines broke. People were not told this until after they were "delivered."

We are 38,000 feet above sea level, cruising along at 523 miles per hour. How many miles have we flown in eight hours and five minutes? In another hour and twenty minutes, we are scheduled to be in Atlanta. Now we are over York and getting close to Pennsylvania. Air flight is still a miracle to me! From DFW to Atlanta, Vienna, Salzburg, Munich, Oberammergau, Innsbruck, the Black Forest, Basel, Bern, Vermaat, Interlaken, Luzern, and Zurich, we have traveled many miles. We are ready for home and family.

Epilogue: Dad's Garden

The packet, a legal-sized brown envelope, which had definitely seen better days, came into my possession some years ago. Its contents had been a puzzle to me for quite some time: an old pocket watch with fob and chain, the stone with the message written on it, a very long letter from my grandfather, parts of which were almost indecipherable, and a family history compiled by Helen Jean Pauley Bickers with artwork by Barbara Faye Pauley Cope.

He was born to James Iverson Pauley and Rozena Miller Pauley on October 12, 1891, and had three older brothers, four younger brothers, and three sisters. His family lived near Yawkey in Lincoln County, West Virginia, and made a meager living by farming and keeping a few head of livestock for food. Occasionally the family sold or traded a cow or pig for other supplies that were needed.

The school building was so far away that the boys didn't go to school until they were about twelve years old. Daniel finished the eighth grade and enlisted in the army. He was in the infantry and was sent to France where he served until the war ended on November 18, 1918. While in the service, he served as a cook, but he still had some close calls. He stayed on in Germany and attended Bonn University, majoring in elementary education. Upon returning to the United States, he immediately got his teaching certificate and was hired to teach school on Bull Creek in Boone County. Daniel taught there about two years and saved enough money to buy a piece of property in Madison and promptly moved his aging parents from Lincoln County so he could see to their well-being.

A short, stocky man, Daniel was every inch a gentleman. He had blue eyes that looked as if God had dipped a paintbrush in the sky and painted them. His hair was black and well groomed. His ancestors were Irish and English.

Daniel felt restless and decided to try something different. He had heard of a mine opening up at Ethel, and on Saturday, he packed his satchel and headed there on foot. It's about thirty miles from Madison to Ethel by car, but by crossing a couple of mountains, he could make it by dark if he kept moving.

That night, Daniel stopped at a boardinghouse in Ethel and inquired about the availability of a room. The owner called for one of the girls to show Mr. Pauley to his room and also where he could wash up for supper. No one ate at this table with unwashed hands, and no one left the table hungry.

The girl looked more like a vision than a real one. She certainly was beautiful. He had known a lot of girls slightly and one or two a little better, but this girl was different. After eating and inquiring about the time of the church meeting the next day, he retired for the night. He never missed church if he was able to go.

It was a beautiful Sunday morning, and after a filling breakfast at the boardinghouse, he was off to church. Perhaps the young girl he had met briefly the night before would be there. As soon as he was inside the church, he looked around hurriedly and decided to sit on the back pew. The preacher was the traveling kind and was only in town one Sunday a month. Being a dedicated Freewill Baptist, he took his time about preaching. After a couple of hours on those hard benches in mid-July Daniel was relieved to hear the last Amen.

Just as he was going up the steps of the boardinghouse, he caught a glimpse of the girl going in the back door. She sure was a pretty girl, but there was something else about her. She saw him looking at her and hurriedly put on an apron and started dishing up Sunday dinner for the boarders. A fine dinner it was too. He had never before eaten such biscuits. He went to the kitchen door and asked to speak to one of the cooks. He was going to express his pleasure for such a fine meal. The pretty young girl turned from the stove and asked what he wanted. "I just wanted to thank you for the fine meal ..." and suddenly he was unable to go on. She seemed shy, but one couldn't really be sure.

Finally he found his voice again and told her he looked for her at church this morning. Her reply really surprised him. "Them Freewills make too much noise, and besides Poppa said we didn't have to go every Sunday. They carry on like God is deaf, especially Aunt Lizzy. Me and my sister can hear her stomping her feet clear over to our house. Poppa said she could save a lot of shoe leather by sitting on her *bench and clapping her hands over her mouth. Poppa said—"*

Daniel interrupted her and told her he would like to meet her poppa.

She told him that Poppa was sitting on the back porch. Poppa did a lot of sitting on the back porch on Sundays. Daniel went around the house and found the situation just as she had described it.

The letter and family history seemed to be interwoven, but only the letter contained information about the objects in the envelope. Though each of the items was interesting in itself, the stone was perhaps the most intriguing of all. From his letter, I learned that the stone came into his possession during the time of the Matewan Massacre.

Many miners at Matewan were interested in becoming part of a union so they could earn higher wages. The mine company had hired detectives to "discourage" miners from joining the union and to eject those who did join the union from company housing. So many miners were ejected from working in the mines it became necessary to hire "scab labor" (black men and others who would work for less money). These men set up tents near Matewan because they couldn't live in company housing, and they were greatly resented by those whom they were replacing.

The situation was already intense when lead Detective Delts got a warrant for the arrests of some union sympathizers. Sheriff Hatfield, who sympathized with the miners, was one of the men to be arrested. He was trying to get a warrant to arrest Detective Delts. When Delts came to serve his warrants, there was a melee, and Delts and several other detectives were killed. Miners began looking for the scabs with violent intentions. There were skirmishes, one of which resulted in a black man being beaten badly before he escaped. He momentarily collapsed near the house Daniel had built for himself and his new bride.

"Loli, I believe there's somebody out there in the road who has been hurt," he said as he peered out the window. "I'm going to see if he needs help."

"Daniel, if he's a scab, they'll kill us for helping him," Lola breathlessly replied.

"It doesn't matter if he's a scab or not, he needs help. He's hurt!" Daniel helped the bleeding man to his feet and brought him into the house, tending to his facial wounds as he did so. As soon as they got inside the house, Daniel doused the lantern light. "If they don't see a light, maybe they'll think we're sleeping."

"Daniel, he's a black man! If they find him here, they'll do the same thing to us they were doing to him."

"I know that," he whispered. "So they mustn't find him."

Moans from the man sounded as loud as thunder, though they must have been only whimpers. There were sounds like someone or something was moving around outside. Flickering lamps could be seen through the window, and there followed a loud thumping on the door.

"Open up in there," a rather loud, boisterous, and perhaps drunken man yelled. "We've got business with you! This is Detective Pitts, and we're looking for a darkie scab on the run. Open up."

Timidly Daniel cracked the door open a few inches and asked, "What's happening out there?"

"There's been a massacre in town. Seven mine detectives were killed. Sheriff Hatfield has been arrested, and we're rounding up scabs. We chased one this way because he run off when we wuz interrogatin' him. You seen him?"

"Seems like I did see something hurrying yonder toward the woods a little while ago, but I couldn't be sure who or what it was."

"If he's in the woods, we'll git him." The man's breath was so heavy with whiskey Daniel figured he could have started a fire if he had struck a match. "You better lock your doors. It wouldn't do for one of those scabs to git into somebody's house, no sir, not for the scab or the people in the house."

Daniel wondered if the man intended some insinuation, and he felt a twinge of guilt because he hadn't told the full truth. He had seen the Negro man headed for the woods, but he had also seen him collapse and had brought him into the house. After the detectives had wandered off into the woods, Daniel again checked on the wounded victim. The bleeding had stopped, and the beating victim seemed to be breathing better. His eyes were open, and they followed Daniel around the room. His voice creaked and he said, "Sir, I can't stay here."

"You really don't have a choice," replied Daniel. "Right now, detectives are scouring the area like hunters looking for squirrels. Wait a day or two. Rest, eat some of Loli's cooking, and you'll be strong enough to leave."

And so he was. On the third day, before the sun rose enough to shed light on the day, he slipped quietly out and away. He had said his thanks and prayed God's blessings on the Pauleys the evening before so that he could sleep in the woodshed and leave before other people would be out and about.

As Daniel prepared to leave for work at his sawmill (he supplied timber for the mines), he prayed that all had gone well for the man. Soon a visitor caused him to question if all had gone well.

Just as Daniel was leaving his front porch, Detective Pitts came huffing and puffing from the woods toward Daniel's house, his rifle resting in the crook of his arm. "Hold up there, Mr. Pauley. I've got some definite business with you."

"Lord, help us," Daniel breathed to himself. "How can I help you, Detective?"

"It's about someone you may have already helped, Mr. Pauley. What I don't know is if it was on purpose or accidental. I've watched your house the past two mornings, sir. Saw you leave for work yesterday. Saw a shadowy figure near your woodshed this morning. He lit out for the woods. He was a good bit in front of me, but I got a good shot at him, and I think I must have hit him pretty good. He sure did yell pretty loud. Thought I might take you up there with me to get the body before you go to work. You can maybe explain how this man was around your house—and you didn't even know it. Can you explain that?"

"No, sir. I can't," Daniel replied as earnestly as possible. "I don't think anyone has been in my woodshed for two days, but I haven't needed any wood or tools the past two days. I haven't been in the shed myself."

"Well, maybe the feller will still be alive when we get there and he can tell us himself. Let's go please." The detective slowly lifted his rifle and pointed it at Daniel. "Walk ahead of me please."

Myriad thoughts passed through Daniel's mind as they trudged together toward the woods. After they entered the woods, the detective poked him with the end of the rifle as he directed, telling Daniel which way to go. They were just beginning to ascend a little hill when he told Daniel to stop.

"This is about where I was when I shot him. He was between that big oak and the boulder when he went down. We'll just ease on up kinda careful now in case he's still alive and kicking."

As they approached the boulder from below, bits of rock and dirt began to fall from above.

"Careful, now," said the detective. "We wouldn't want to get hit by a rock now, would we?"

Daniel saw the stone hurtling toward the detective, but he didn't see how it was launched or by whom. As Pitts turned to see what Daniel was looking at, the stone hit him squarely on the side of the head, knocking him to the ground. Pitts didn't move. Stunned, Daniel picked up the stone, put it in his pocket, moved to the prone body of Detective Pitts, and felt for a pulse. There was a fairly strong pulse, but Daniel knew that Pitts still needed help.

Atop the boulder, Daniel saw the outline of a man peering down in their direction. The man gave a brief wave as he retreated from the boulder, using a small tree limb as a cane and walking gingerly.

Using his pocketknife, Daniel cut some saplings, put together a crude stretcher, and pulled the detective's body to the sawmill. Daniel was short and stocky, but he was also strong. At the saw mill, he hitched the stretcher to one of his mules and rode the mule to the office of the company doctor.

Pitts had regained consciousness, but he was really confused. His head felt like a drum with the skin stretched too tight. He kept uttering, "Where's the body?" and "Avalanche!"

Daniel had some questions of his own, which he kept to himself. In years to come, he would tell the story many times, never mentioning the name or race of the scab who was beaten—until he wrote the notes for Joe. He always included the "stone that came from above."

It was the stone, which was included in the packet, the stone on which the words "Dad's Garden" were inscribed. Because of that stone and the one who "launched it," Dad lived long enough to have children and grandchildren (his garden) of which I was one. Who is to say it wasn't God who caused that stone to be launched?

Several more questions plagued my mind after receiving the packet. What was the man's name? How long did he live? Was he married? Did he have children or grandchildren? How many lives have been affected because Dad and Mom Pauley helped him in a time of need?

To this very day, that stone sits atop a dresser surrounded by pictures of our two children (Matthew Joseph and Meredith Leigh) and their children (Julia Michelle, Alexandria Leigh, Hannah Noel, Autumn Elizabeth, Caden Eli, and Morgan Victoria) with Matt's wife (Tara) and Meredith's husband (Casey Wiley).

Into whose possession will the stone pass when Sondra and I have died and gone to heaven? Only God knows—and he's not telling.